Secrets of the Undead

My Life Among the Undead:
Book 3

Camara M. Bragdon

Printed in the United States of America.

For more information, or to book an event, contact :
www.camarambragdonauthor.com

Book design by Camara M. Bragdon
Cover design by Camara M. Bragdon

ISBN - 978-1-964265-02-5

My Life Among the Undead

book series!

Friend of the Undead

Yard Sale of the Undead

DEDICATION

This book is dedicated to my small but mighty army of editors: Charlene Randall, Jane Bennett, and Patricia Allen.

CHAPTERS

Chapter One
I Get Offered a Unique Opportunity

My boyfriend has lots of secrets. Little did I know that his biggest one would almost kill me.

It started as a typical day at the Zephyr Public Library. I, Shelly Anderson, human and librarian extraordinaire, was on the fourth floor in the history section shelving a cartload of books when I heard over the intercom system, "Shelly to the front desk! Shelly to the front desk!" I checked my watch. I still had an hour to go before breaks started. This was strange, but then again, Zephyr was a strange town. Strange isn't exactly the right word to describe Zephyr. This city-state crawls with magic and the supernatural. Seeing satyrs and elves riding winged horses and dragons is a common occurrence. Every mythological creature you can think of resides here.

Maybe they need help at the front desk, I thought to myself. I unloaded the pile of books onto the cart I had placed in the middle of the aisle. In a sluggish mood, I decided to take the elevator down to the second floor to the adult circulation desk. Once I reached my destination, I found my supervisor helping a patron apply for a library card. "Yes, Raquel?" I asked the beautiful werewolf in her human form.

"Oh, Shelly, Mrs. Yougha would like to see you in her office," Raquel Lupus answered me as soon as she finished with the patron.

An expression of shock came over my face. Maude Yougha, the head of the library, wanted to see me! Was I in trouble? I tried to read the werewolf's mind, but I was afraid of the consequences. Technically, the Were folk aren't undead, but since they only turn into their animal form at night, they fall into that category. I'm so glad that I can control my limited telepathic abilities. "I'll go see her now."

A few minutes later, I was sitting in a comfortable chair across from Mrs. Yougha, who handed me a letter. "Shelly, I would like you to read this," the enchantress told me as she leaned across her cherry executive desk. Yes, I did say, "enchantress." Mrs. Yougha is a part of a magical race called Welkies. These humans possess various magical abilities and are more commonly known as wizards, enchantresses, sorcerers, and witches. Because Welkies age more slowly than the average human and can live on for centuries, the director is most likely in her late sixties but doesn't look a day over thirty. I perused the letter, not recognizing the college emblem at the top. "But it's during summer break. Does Urbana College of Magic need a head librarian right now?"

Mrs. Yougha smiled at me with her perfectly straight teeth. "Well, Shelly, their last librarian just quit without giving notice. President Blackstone told me that the librarian was in the process of ordering some updated materials for the incoming freshmen."

I was still unsure why the director was telling me this.

Unfortunately, I can only read the minds of the undead, so I would have to get a verbal answer. "I don't understand, Mrs. Yougha," I said.

"Well, I understand that you have expressed interest in working at different kinds of libraries." She got up to smooth out the wrinkles in her navy blue and white pinstripe dress.

I nodded. I had mentioned the idea to Raquel when I started working at the library about three years ago. Even though I really like working in the public library setting, I've also enjoyed the prospect of working in other libraries. "Is it a transfer?"

The enchantress shook her head and laughed. "Oh, no, it's only temporary. You'll only be there for about two weeks, and you'll be paid for your time there."

"It sounds fascinating."

"Well, Urbana College of Magic is a small but very prestigious university in Urbana, a small town about a two-hour train ride. I received my master's degree in library and information science. Unfortunately, the school only accepts Welkies."

Prestigious, maybe, but pretentious! I'm a human but not

a Welkie. I'm from another reality altogether. So, why am I telepathic? Whenever humans enter the magical land of Zephyr through various wormholes that open up between realities, they acquire a magical talent. I can read the minds of the undead and telecommunicate with them. My boyfriend can explain it much better than I can. The school seemed a bit prejudiced, but I was willing to give it a shot. What harm could it do? "I accept the offer!"

"Good, if you could just stay for a few minutes, Shelly, and let me call President Blackstone," Mrs. Yougha said as she began to dial the phone. I barely paid attention as she talked to the person on the other end of the phone line. Finally, she hung up and turned to me. "President Blackstone said that you can start next week."

When I got off work that evening, I stopped by Food & More, the local grocery store. I was in the snack aisle when I ran into my roommate, Lisa Miller. She was getting five bags of chips off the shelves. "Hey, Lisa," I called her.

Lisa stopped checking out her newly dyed blonde hair in her compact mirror and turned to face me. "Have a good day at work?" she asked.

"Yeah," I replied, "I accepted a temporary position at a college library starting next week." I paused to eye the cartload of soda, frozen pizza, and cookies. "Holy crap, Lisa! Are you feeding an army?"

Lisa laughed. "No, I'm feeding the guys. It's band night tonight." The guys included our two brothers, Robin and Roger, my boyfriend's brother, Dirk, a weretiger named Tucker Tigris, and a satyr named Strider Hornsby. Last week, they recruited Lisa to help with the light show when they perform. When my childhood friend and her family came to Zephyr, Lisa acquired the ability to control light particles. The guys, especially Dirk, are impressed with the possibility of a free light show. "They asked me to bring some food," Lisa answered.

"I hope they're paying you back."

"They said they would. If they don't, I'll beat it out of them." She changed the subject. "What are you doing here? I thought you had a date with Eddie tonight."

I grabbed a couple of bags of peanut butter cookies off the shelf. "Oh, I do. I'm having dinner at his house."

"Is he cooking?"

"I think so. I offered to bring a dessert."

Lisa gave me a skeptical look. "I thought you offered to make a dessert." She nodded, her green eyes narrowing in thought. "You were talking to him last night, and you said you would make something 'yummy,' if I may quote you, Shelly."

I gave a nervous laugh. "Yeah, about that! I forgot all about it. Technically, I *made* money to buy the cookies. So, somewhere along the line, I did make them."

Lisa decided she was done shopping for the guys, and we both headed for the checkout line. "So, what are your plans for this evening?"

"Dinner and cookies!" I held up my quick dessert. "Then probably a movie and maybe a couple of games. I don't know. Eddie's the one who pulled this together."

I helped Lisa put her items on the conveyor belt at the checkout. After she paid about sixty druci (the Zephyrian currency) for the entire purchase, she watched the elfin cashier

charge $2.59 to my debit card and shook her head. "Maybe I

should have just bought cookies."

I laughed. "Guys are bottomless pits. That's why I bought

two packages of cookies. I've got to get going." I waved goodbye

to her. "I'll be home late tonight, most likely. So, don't wait up."

We went our separate ways, me to my winged horse, Jordan,

and she to her gentle, purple dragon, Lucky.

I changed into a clean pair of blue jeans and a dark green

sweater before I headed over to my boyfriend's place. Then I

looked at the packages of cookies sitting on my kitchen table. It

would look tacky if I brought them in the cellophane wrapper. It

took me a few minutes to find the pretty plastic tray I had

confiscated from my dad about a year ago. I may not be a good

cook, but my cookie arrangements are spectacular. Opening

both packages, I layered the cookies until they made three

circles, one inside another. I placed two layers of saran wrap

tightly over the tray. The last thing I needed was the cookies

falling all over the place. I stood back to admire my creation.

Gathering up my purse, I headed out the door to Jordan while I balanced the tray in one hand.

My winged horse whinnied impatiently as I set the tray down on the grass next to the wooden cross-shaped post. Jordan fluttered her broad chocolate brown wings and nearly knocked me over as I untied her reins. Thankfully, Jordan didn't buck or jump as I set the tray on her back. I carefully climbed on, and with one hand on the platter, I ordered, "To the Van Helsing home!"

The green, three-story mansion rose high, casting a beautiful shadow against the gorgeous painted orange and purple sky. We landed on the perfectly trimmed lawn right by a post that Eddie had rigged up just for my horse. My boyfriend lives with his brother in the old mansion. I dismounted and tied Jordan's reins to the post without dropping the cookie tray. I opened up the front door and stepped inside the front hallway. My boyfriend had told me to let myself in when I got there. "Eddie, it's Shelly!" I called.

"In the kitchen!" Eddie called back.

It took me a few seconds to walk to the kitchen. Standing in front of the stove back to me was my boyfriend, Eddie Van Helsing. The vampire stopped stirring the pasta that was steaming in a medium-sized pot and turned to face me. "Hey, Shell," he said as he gave me a fanged smile. "You're here a bit early, aren't you?" He gave me a quick kiss on the cheek, which nearly made my toes curl. He eyed the tray in my hands. "And you brought cookies. I'll take those off your hands."

"Unfortunately, they're store-bought," I told Eddie as I watched him set the tray on the black island counter in the middle of the kitchen. *Wow,* I thought to myself as I stared at him in his maroon casual shirt and dark blue jeans, *I can't believe that I'm dating a hot-looking vampire who cooks!* "Hey, do you need any help with dinner?"

Eddie shook his head of jet-black, curly hair. "No, thanks, I've got it all under control, Shelly. You sit back and relax. Help yourself to the cream soda in the fridge."

Give me a bottle of cream soda, and I'm yours. I pulled open the refrigerator door and pushed away the bottles of various fruit juices. Both Eddie and his brother, Dirk, are vegetarian vampires, and so I've never found a bottle of blood in their house unless it was for one of their blood-drinking relatives. "You want something, too?" I offered Eddie as I grabbed a bottle of cream soda.

"I'm fine," he replied. I don't usually read the minds of the undead on purpose, but I read Eddie's mind without thinking. He was making us a country vegetable pasta salad seasoned with fresh pineapple juice but wanted to surprise me.

Just as I found that out, he blocked my telepathy. "Hey, hey, hey!" he protested playfully. "No mind-reading! I wanted the dinner to be a surprise." Vampires are the only people who can block telepathy, and I hated it when Eddie did that.

"Sorry about that!" I said. I tucked a piece of my long brown hair behind my ear. Flying in the open air can mess up your hair. I wanted to make sure my hair looked all right. "I'm going to use your bathroom."

"Okay, dinner will be ready in a few minutes," Eddie said as he emptied the pasta into a magical strainer that hovered over the sink. I had to get myself one of those.

I walked into the bathroom next to the kitchen. The bathroom was about the size of a closet with a toilet, a sink, and—. "Oh, crap!" I said.

"What's wrong?" Eddie called from the kitchen.

"There's no mirror in here."

"You're in a house owned by vampires. What do you expect?"

"A mirror in the bathroom."

Eddie came into the bathroom. When he noticed me attempting to fix my disheveled hair, he ran his slender fingers through my hair. I *love* it when the vampire does that. "Your hair looks just fine, babe," he assured me. He had started calling me babe only last week. Unfortunately, I hadn't come up with a pet name for him that doesn't involve rhyming words that start with "w." Nothing would turn the vampire off more, than if I started calling him my little schnookums wookums.

"Thanks, Eddie, but still, you should at least put up a mirror when you have visitors over," I said.

He grinned at me. "I'll keep that in mind," he replied as we walked back to the kitchen. "Dinner's on the table, but first, I want to put away the dishes that I washed earlier today."

I looked around at the stack of pots and pans that were piled high on the dish rack next to the two chrome sinks. Eddie had left them to drip dry all day. I didn't want to sit on my duff while the vampire cleaned up the kitchen. "Need some help?" I asked.

He shook his head. "No thanks, Shell, I've got it!" He faced both of his palms toward the dishes. "Borax pots!" he commanded in a rapid tone. Suddenly, the dishes began flying around the kitchen. A cupboard door swung open just above my head and slammed shut as a pot flung inside. "Oh, crap!" the vampire said.

A skillet came flying straight at us. "Eddie, look out!" I cried. Suddenly I was pushed to the linoleum floor. The frying pan darted into an opened cupboard right above our heads. I tried to get up, but my boyfriend was on top of me. "Get off of me," I ordered him.

Eddie rolled off, barely missing a saucepan that whizzed

over my body. "Don't get up!" he told me as its matching cover

followed close by into another cupboard.

"What the heck did you do?" I demanded as a cupboard

door behind me swung open and smacked my head.

"I said a cleaning spell too fast."

"No kidding, Sherlock. Can you stop the freaking spell?"

Eddie shook his head. "The spell only goes on for a few

minutes."

Great, I thought to myself. *Just what I wanted! I could

picture the headlines now. Librarian killed by flying frying pan;

Police suspect boyfriend error.* I lay flat on the ground as the last

pot put itself in a cupboard above the sink.

The vampire got up from the floor and then pulled me to

my feet. "Did I hurt you when I pushed you to the floor?" he

asked. "I'm so sorry, Shelly!"

"Eddie, I'm fine," I replied. "Don't ever do that spell

again!"

"It's a harmless spell, babe, unless you say it too fast like I

did!" He laughed nervously. He knew that I was not pleased with

his little mishap. "That's why I don't do that spell very often."

"That spell nearly killed me. Just be more careful next time you do it." I gave him a big hug to let him know that I wasn't mad at him. He led me into the little dining room. A big smile broke out on my face the moment I saw the two candles at one end of the table. Eddie had bought a brand-new, white tablecloth just for this occasion. He even used the good china for our meal. "Eddie, what's the occasion?" I asked as I sat down in the chair that he pulled out for me. I placed the white cloth napkin across my lap.

"Nothing! Can't a guy make a romantic dinner for his girl without any particular reason?" The vampire's green eyes twinkled mischievously at me. He waved his right palm over the top of the two candles and said in a soft voice, "Nebulae." A small ball of white fire about the size of a ping-pong ball appeared suddenly over his fingertips. He lit the candles and made the fire disappear. He walked over to the light switch and cast the dining room into darkness with only our candles giving off a warm glow. "What do you think?" he asked me.

My hands covered my face as I began blushing. The

vampire had pulled this entire evening together just because.

"It's great, Eddie. It's more than great! It's wonderful!"

Eddie uncorked a bottle of sparkling grape cider and poured about half of it into my wine glass and his. Neither one of us drinks alcohol, but pouring anything from a two-liter soda bottle into fancy crystal goblets is just plain tacky. That's why he bought two bottles of sparkling cider for our date. "One or two spoonfuls?" he asked me, referring to the pasta salad in a delicate crystal serving bowl.

"Two, please!"

My boyfriend gave me two heaping scoops of country vegetable pasta salad with a splash of pineapple juice. Then he served himself. As we ate, I asked him how his day went. "Good, I slept until around three worked out in the garage for about an hour, and then made dinner."

"Ooh, did you fix your bike?" I asked Eddie. He had gotten a flat tire on his motorcycle last week. If there's one thing that everyone in Zephyr knows about the vampire, it's that he's always riding around on his bike. He's a great mechanic, and when he's not working the night shift at my dad's diner, you can always find him under one of his eight cars tinkering with something. But the motorcycle is his favorite mode of transportation. "Can we go for a ride?" I asked

He shook his head. "Can't. I found out that I have to repair a crack in the exhaust pipe. Some other time, babe." He took a sip of cider. "So, how was your day at work?"

"I've been offered a temporary job." I then told Eddie about my conversation with Mrs. Yougha. The vampire's brow was furrowed in thought as I talked. For some reason, he wasn't pleased with my news.

"You didn't accept, did you?" he asked.

"I did. What's wrong with that?"

Eddie hesitated and looked away from me. "Nothing!" he murmured. Something had upset him, so I decided to use my magical talent to figure out what was going on. But Eddie was blocking my telepathy. "I heard that something bad happened there, and I don't want you to get hurt."

His concern was touching, but something wasn't right. Eddie wasn't telling me everything, but I got the feeling that he didn't want to talk about it, whatever it was. I decided to leave it alone. The atmosphere for the rest of the evening had changed. While snuggling up against Eddie on the couch, I noticed that he was absentmindedly stroking my hair as we watched a crime drama on television. I wanted to ask him what was wrong but decided not to mention it when I saw the faraway look in his eyes. About eleven o'clock, I finally left the Van Helsing home with unanswered questions and an upset boyfriend.

Chapter Two
The Healing Power of Cake

The following night Jordan and I flew to my dad's house.

Dad had invited me over for dinner earlier. When I arrived, I saw

that my brother's dragon, my dad's giant eagle, and Lisa's

dragon were already in the backyard. I didn't have to worry about

the dragons or the eagle taking off with Jordan in their talons

since the dragons are no bigger than she is, and my dad's

Tradewinds only eats rats and mice which is fine by me. I tied

the winged horse's reins to a nearby tree, trudged up the back

porch steps, and opened the sliding glass door that led into the

living room.

My brother, Robin, was sitting in the brown leather

armchair. Even though he is only a year older than I am, my

brother has been climbing the career ladder at the Zephyr police

station. He was studying for the detective exam when I walked in. "Okay, Rog, give me another question," he said to the tall, red-headed district attorney.

Roger Miller, a guy I grew up with, crushed peanuts in his hand as he read from the book on his lap. "'A Welkie is found in possession of a gargoyle. The gargoyle destroyed both the neighbor's property and his own. What charges would be filed against him?'"

Robin closed his deep blue eyes in thought. "Did the wizard know that the gargoyle was illegal? Because if he didn't know about it, then I would have to arrest him for criminal negligence."

Twenty-seven-year-old Roger began grinding the peanut deeper into the palm of his hand. "Don't read into it! Just answer the freaking question, Robin!" he said in a frustrated tone. Because Roger and Lisa are from the same reality as my family, he can mentally manipulate objects on a molecular level. Today, he was venting his frustration with my brother by using his molecukinesis to make the peanuts whole and then crushing it over and over again.

Robin opened his mouth to answer the question when he

saw me. "Hey, Shelly, the next time you talk to Eddie, can you tell him that we need to reschedule poker night because I have to study for the detective exam that night?" he asked.

"Sure," I replied with a nod. "I'll try to remember that." Eddie's behavior last night had me worried all day, but I hadn't told anybody about it. No need to worry the guys, especially Robin, who was attempting to become the youngest detective in the history of Zephyr's police force. I walked into the kitchen as Roger snapped his fingers to get my brother back on track.

My dad and his friend, Bruce Miller, were in the kitchen. I sat on a barstool at the counter next to Lisa as she helped the beautiful, thirty-eight-year-old Amelia Cross plan the upcoming marriage to my father. "How are the wedding plans coming along?" I asked them in an attempt to take my mind off of Eddie.

Amelia and Lisa stopped talking and looked at me. "Shelly, you got home really late last night," Lisa said with a wink. "How was dinner?"

"Good," I replied.

Amelia looked at Lisa and then at me. "Mind telling me

what's going on, girls?" she asked.

"Eddie made dinner for Shelly last night at his place," Lisa announced.

Dad and Bruce turned to look at me. "Wow, Shelly! I'm impressed with your boyfriend!" Dad said, crossing his arms. "What was the occasion?"

"Just because." I then told them about the romantic dinner the vampire had made for me. I glanced at some of the flower arrangement brochures that Lisa was showing Amelia. My friend had been hired as their wedding planner.

"See, Bruce?" Dad said as he scooped the mashed potatoes into a huge serving bowl. "I told you Eddie's a good guy!"

Bruce gave a non-committal grunt. The gray and red-headed cook doesn't like Eddie per se. Bruce tolerates my boyfriend like one tolerates an ingrown toenail. He thinks that Eddie is no good for me and has told Dad that on several occasions. But since Eddie and Bruce both work for my dad, they attempt to get along.

"Timothy," Amelia asked my dad, "how come you never

make me a romantic dinner just because?"

Dad smiled at Amelia. Using his elasticity ability, he reached around the corner and swatted at Amelia's backside with a hand towel. "I did, darling!" he told her. "When I proposed to you two months ago."

Amelia pushed a piece of her short, black hair behind her ear. "That was a special occasion." She turned to me. "Perhaps, Eddie can teach your father some romance tips," she whispered.

"I think Dad does a pretty good job," I replied with a smile. I was looking forward to my dad's second wedding. Dad had a great marriage to my mom before she died when I was thirteen. Amelia brought back that spark of life into my dad's baby blue eyes when they first met. Even though I had already been asked to be one of the bridesmaids, I wanted to help make their wedding special. "Have you picked out wedding invitations yet?" I asked them.

Lisa nodded. "Amelia and I thought that you could design the template for invitations."

"I would love to," I replied. I love to draw and paint. My

artwork has been shown in various art galleries around Zephyr. Even Eddie once risked his life when my paintings were stolen by a kingpin sorcerer in Zephyr. I gave a great sigh when I thought of my boyfriend's attitude last night.

"Everything all right, Shelly?" Dad asked.

"I don't know, Dad," I answered. "Eddie was acting weird last night."

My friend gasped. "Is he going to ask you to marry him?" she asked. "Can I plan the wedding?"

"Whoa! Whoa!" I said, holding up my hands. "Let's not start any rumors here, Lisa. I mentioned my new job to Eddie, and he kind of flipped out."

"What new job?" Dad asked. He and Bruce finished setting the rest of the food on the table. "Boys," he shouted to Robin and Roger. "Time to eat!"

Once everyone had sat down, I told them about the meeting with the library director. "So, when I told Eddie about it, he got quiet and told me that he didn't want me to go."

"Why?" Robin asked. "That doesn't sound like Eddie."

"I know," I said. "You'd think he'd be happy for me." As I

talked, my hands got very animated. I gasped in horror as my hand hit my glass full of grape juice. The dark liquid spilled onto the white tablecloth and my brand-new khaki capris. "I'm so sorry, Dad!"

"It's okay, Shelly!" Dad replied.

"Oh, crap! These pants are ruined." I grabbed the paper napkin and dabbed at the considerable spot. Klutz, in action, that's me!

Robin, who was sitting next to me, held his napkin up to his face. His entire body was shaking with laughter. After three more minutes of him snorting and chuckling, he got a hold of himself. "I'm sorry, Shelly. You were saying?"

Roger shook his head. "He hasn't slept in four days! I've been helping him study for his detective exam. And the D.A. wonders why I've been coming into work tired every morning." Roger and Robin were not only best friends but roommates as well. I was getting the feeling that the young prosecutor was about to kill my brother if Robin didn't get some sleep and stopped annoying him.

"Anyway," I said, "when I tried to read Eddie's mind, he blocked it."

"It sounds like he's becoming very controlling, Shelly," Bruce said in a prophetic tone.

"No, it wasn't that. Something was troubling Eddie. He got distant, and we didn't talk about it for the rest of the night. I didn't want to upset him. He was down."

"Maybe he had trouble sleeping," Lisa suggested. "I bet even vampires can have off days."

"But I've never seen him like this before," I answered. I care a lot for Eddie, and it hurts me to see him so upset. I rested my head on my closed fist and shut my eyes. "Can we change the subject?" I asked. My thoughts were elsewhere as Dad and Bruce talked about Bruce's love interest, an elf by the name of Libby Elfstar, who was working as a waitress in my dad's diner. Maybe Lisa was right, and Eddie would be acting like himself tomorrow.

I didn't hear from Eddie for the next two days. Every time I called him, I was asked to leave a message on his voicemail. It seemed like he was avoiding me, but I couldn't figure out why. After I finished the eighth message, I decided to stop so that no one could accuse me of stalking him. The evening before leaving for my new job, I came home from work and threw my green and white canvas bag on the kitchen table. Lisa looked up from jotting something down on a slip of pink lined paper. There were three neatly stacked piles of papers surrounding her seat. "Careful, Shelly," my roommate admonished. "I just separated the three weddings that I'm doing into these piles."

"Sorry," I said as I grabbed a bottle of soda out of the fridge. I glanced at our landline phone. There was a big red zero blinking on the answering machine. "Hey, did we get any messages?"

"None from Eddie, if that's what you wanted," Lisa replied. She handed me the piece of paper that she was writing on. "Here is a list of design ideas that Amelia wants on the invitations. She wants you to pick out a few and put together a simple design."

I sat down and looked at the paper. Amelia had picked out

a light hue of royal blue and silver for the wedding colors. I was thankful that it wasn't red or green because the big day was going to happen in the first week of December. Robin, who can control and animate plant life, was going to be in charge of setting up all the morning glories and baby's breath for the wedding. "I haven't had any time to think about the invitations," I replied.

"You've been thinking about Eddie, aren't you?"

I nodded. "He hasn't returned any of my calls."

"How many times did you call him?"

"Eight."

Lisa's jaw dropped in shock. "If you weren't dating him, I'd call that stalking."

"So would he," I replied with a weary smile.

Lisa got up from the table. She grabbed her black leather designer purse. "You know what, Shelly?" She grabbed my hand and pulled me to my feet. "We need to celebrate your new job properly."

"And where do you propose we go?"

"To Natalie's Sweet House."

About half an hour later, Lisa and I were back at my place with a day-old marble swirl cake that read "Happy Birthday to One of My Best Girls, Betty." The two-inch thick snow-white frosting was smothered with cute little red and purple sugar rosettes.

Most likely, Betty was beating the crap out of the guy who ordered the cake for her and wasn't going to get a chance to eat any of this delicious cake that could serve at least six people. I took two plates from the china cabinet while Lisa got a knife, a spoon and a fork. (The spoon was for me. I know I'm weird, but I like to eat cake with a spoon.) As I bit into the cakey goodness, I realized that we needed to share this scrumptious dessert with someone who is very yummy, to me, at least.

My cell phone rang. "Hello, Eddie!" I said.

"Hey, Shell!" my boyfriend said.

"Did you get my messages?"

"Yes, all eight of them," he said with a laugh. "Shelly, I'm fine. I'm sorry if I worried you. I just had a bad day."

I shrugged. I didn't believe that the vampire was telling me the whole truth, but I didn't want to push the issue. "Whatcha up to?" I asked as I loaded my spoon with more cake.

"Fixing the muffler on the 'picklemobile' as you like to call it." Eddie owns about eight cars all in different shapes of fruits and vegetables and a motorcycle, but the 'picklemobile' is my all-time favorite car. The car is shaped like a deep green pickle and looks like it has been a few scrapes with Godzilla. I swear he has dumped more money into that rattling machine than someone puts down for a house mortgage.

"Again? Eddie, you've got to get rid of that thing."

"You like the picklemobile."

"No, I like making fun of the picklemobile."

"Once I put this muffler in place, this baby will purr like a kitten."

"A kitten in mid-strangulation, maybe! Anyway, Lisa and I are eating a birthday cake right now, and I wanted to invite you over for a piece."

Eddie paused. "I don't know, Shelly. I have to—Wait, did you say 'cake'?"

"With extra frosting!"

"Oh, I'm there! See you in a few!"

True to his word, Lisa and I heard my boyfriend's motorcycle roaring up our driveway. I opened the door and let Eddie inside. "Wow! That was fast!" I told him as I gave him a big hug. "You must have hit all the green lights."

The vampire set his maroon helmet on the kitchen counter. "A few," he said with a shrug. He read the horrified look on my face as I thought he had run some red lights on his way here. "They were all yellow! Red means 'stop,' green means 'go,' and yellow means 'step on the gas.' You've ridden with me before, Shelly. You know the drill."

I rolled my eyes at him. "Come have a piece of cake with us." I grabbed his elbow and had him sit down at the table. Lisa dished out a slice of cake for Eddie as I sat down next to him.

He dug into the overloaded frosted cake. "This is excellent! Where did you get it?" he asked.

"Natalie's Sweet House," Lisa replied as she rinsed off her

plate in the kitchen sink.

Eddie finished off his slice in no time at all. "Guess what I discovered on my newly-waxed carrot car yesterday!" my undead boyfriend said as he helped himself to another piece of cake.

"What?" I asked.

"A big pile of dragon turd!"

Lisa and I began laughing. Dirk's dragon must have had a sudden case of diarrhea, and when Ringo poops, you can smell it a mile away. "How long did you spend waxing the car?" I asked, just to push the envelope.

"Two freaking hours! That was after I spent two additional hours cleaning it off!" Eddie shook his head in frustration. "I took another shower so that Mr. Anderson wouldn't fire me for stinking up the dinner."

Lisa cleaned up her paperwork. "I'm sure it didn't take that long, Eddie."

"Are you kidding?" Eddie said. "That last time Ringo left me a present, it had already hardened, and I spent three hours cleaning it up!"

I nearly gagged on my cake as the mental picture crossed my mind. "Eww, eww! That's disgusting, Eddie."

"I'm sorry, but that's what the stupid dragon did."

"I like dragons," Lisa said. My friend has a crush on Dirk, but since her father doesn't care for vampires, I highly doubt that Lisa wants to incur the wrath of her father.

"Then you and Dirk would get along great," Eddie said to her. He eyed the half-eaten cake hungrily. My boyfriend really wanted another piece but didn't want to turn into a pig, figuratively, of course, in front of our very eyes. Just because he's a vampire doesn't mean he can't eat three pieces of cake with so much frosting it can put a person on a sugar high for weeks.

I cut another piece of the cake and handed it to my boyfriend. "Take another piece, Eddie. I know you want it."

Lisa looked at me. The cake was definitely bigger than we had expected. "Take some home to Dirk. 'Cause once Shelly leaves tomorrow night, I definitely won't be eating it. Which means I have to be good for the rest of the week." Even though she is cheerleader-thin, Lisa's always trying out new diet plans. My favorite diet is the candy-and-ice-cream plan. It's not calories if you eat them from the package.

Eddie got up to leave. He covered the remaining pieces of cake with saran wrap. "Where are you going, Shelly?" he asked with surprise.

"I told you the other night," I said. "I'm going to be working at the Urbana College of Magic library."

"Oh, that!" he said without enthusiasm. "You're still going?" Just by his voice, I knew that he wasn't happy for me. Every time I brought up my new job to him, he would get that faraway look in his eyes.

"Yeah, what's wrong?" I asked, demanding to get some answers.

"Nothing, I just don't want you to go."

"Why?"

"Because—," he paused as he racked his brain for an answer because he wasn't about to tell me the truth. "Because it's too far away. Urbana is over two hours away!"

"Oh, please!" I said. "It's not like I'm moving there. It's only a two-week job!"

"I just think that you getting a job far away isn't good for our relationship right now!"

"Eddie, that's a bunch of crap!" I looked over at Lisa for support. "Isn't that right, Lisa?"

Lisa held up her hands. "Don't get me involved in this lovers' quarrel," she replied. She gathered up her paperwork and walked to her room so Eddie and I could have a moment alone.

I crossed my arms and looked directly into the vampire's eyes. "I thought you'd be happy for me. What aren't you telling me, Eddie?"

My boyfriend set his cake on the little table by my door and wrapped his arms around me. "I'm concerned about your safety."

"I can take care of myself, Eddie." I gave him a tender kiss on the lips. I knew that he meant well, but why was he worried about my safety? What was at the college library to harm me? Killer books? I decided not to ask him again.

"I know you can, Babe. Just be careful while you're there."

He let go of me. "When are you leaving?" he asked as I opened the door for him.

"Dad's dropping me off at the train station at seven."

"Then I'll let you pack. I'll talk to you later, babe," he said. He gave me a quick kiss on the lips and turned to leave when I stopped him.

"You forgot something, Eddie!" I handed him his helmet, which he tucked under his arm, and we waved goodbye to each other. Leaning against the frame of my open front door, I watched as my boyfriend opened the little hatch on the back of his bright green motorcycle. Then he used a minimizer spell on the cake box. The cake shrank to half its size, and he carefully set it inside the hatch. The last thing he wanted was a mashed slice of cake. Then his gorgeous body straddled the motorcycle as he put on his helmet. With a roar of the engine, he sped off into the night.

I stepped back inside. I never want to let Eddie go. He's the most handsome man I have ever met yet the most mysterious. His vast knowledge of magic puzzled me as I locked the door. "He knows all about performing spells, but how does he do it?"

Chapter Three
My First Train Ride

Around six-thirty the next evening, I was sitting in the passenger seat of my father's dark green SUV. Dad rarely drove it since we came to Zephyr. He prefers flying his giant eagle but uses the SUV when he's traveling with more than two people. The engine groaned in protest as Dad shifted gears on the bumpy road. "You should have Eddie look at the engine," I told Dad.

He nodded. "It's the transmission. Eddie looked at it the other night. He said that he would try to repair it this weekend." He glanced at the handwritten directions that I was holding in my hands. "What's our next turn?"

"Left on Madagascar Avenue," I said after I turned on the overhead light. No matter what season it is, the sun always starts to set at six o'clock in the evening. "Turn right now!"

Dad made a sharp turn onto the street. "Speaking of Eddie," he said to me, "how are you two doing?"

I shrugged. "We kind of made up last night," I explained. I am very close to my father, and I can tell him anything. "Eddie just seems worried for my safety, but I don't understand why."

"He cares a lot for you, Shelly."

"I know, but I don't know why he's so worried. I'm not planning on putting myself in any kind of danger."

Dad was quiet for a moment or two. I wished I could tell what he was thinking, but since my telepathy only works with the undead, I would have to wait for my father to tell me what he was thinking. Finally, he spoke, "You know what? I was looking over Eddie's résumé last night, and he went to Urbana College of Magic."

My head whipped around so fast that I felt like Linda Blair. "He did? Why didn't he tell me?"

"I don't know, sweetie. Perhaps something happened at the college, and Eddie probably doesn't want to talk about it. Until your grandfather kicked me out of the house when I was eighteen, I never told anyone that he was a drunken child abuser. Let Eddie bring up his past. Don't pry into it, okay?"

I leaned my head back against the seat. "You're probably right, Dad. I know that Eddie doesn't like to talk about his past. I won't bring it up." The last thing I wanted was to lose my boyfriend because I was a snoop. We finally arrived at the train station. Dad and I got out of the car and unloaded my two rolling suitcases and my laptop shoulder bag from the back seat. As we were about to walk into the station, I heard the familiar roar of a motorcycle engine.

Eddie parked the bike behind the SUV, hung his helmet off the handlebars, and jumped off. "Shelly, wait up!" he called. He sprinted up to us. "I wanted to see you off." He took one of my bags from Dad and attempted to toss it over his shoulder. Even with all of his vampire strength, he struggled under the weight. "God, Shelly, what did you put it here? Bricks?"

"It's not that heavy!" I said as we walked inside. I purchased my round-trip tickets from the dwarf behind the plexiglass ticket counter. "I packed for two weeks," I explained as we walked into the station. People bustled back and forth across the wooden platform, wheeling their suitcases and lugging their briefcases back and forth. Men in business suits kissed and hugged their significant others goodbye before boarding the train. Two centaurs took my bags from Dad and Eddie and put them in the baggage car.

There was a loud blast from the train whistle. A short, overweight elf leaned out the door of one of the passenger cars. "All aboard!" he bellowed. "Last train to Urbana leaves in five minutes!"

"I've got to go! That's my train! I'll call you when I get there, Dad," I said as I gave him a quick hug goodbye.

"Have a good trip, sweetie!" Dad said, returning the hug.

When I turned to hug Eddie, the vampire embraced me tightly. It was as if he didn't want to let me go. "Uh, Eddie!" I said. "I'm going to miss my train!"

"I'm sorry, babe!" He let go of me. "Just be careful, okay?" I nodded. "Call me when you get there!" He gave me a tender kiss on the lips.

"I will. Don't worry, Eddie!" I said with slight

embarrassment. Dad was smiling at us. Forcing myself to pull away from the vampire, I sprinted up the stairs. "Bye, Dad! Bye, Eddie!" I called back to them as the train chugged away. I glanced through the windows to see the two most important men in my life, waving at me. I waved back and nearly lost my balance as the train pulled away from the station.

"Can I help you, miss?" asked the Welkie conductor who looked old enough to be my grandfather.

I nodded my head. "This is my first time on a train," I admitted. "Could you show me where my seat is?" I glanced up and down the two rows of seventies orange bucket seats that lined the passenger car.

He gave me a patronizing smile. "There are no assigned seats on the Sunset Express! You can sit anywhere you want!"

I nodded my thanks while trying to hide my profound embarrassment. God, I felt stupid. I walked down the bright purple carpeted aisle and slipped into one of the leather seats next to the window. The Sunset Express hadn't done well on last year's fundraiser to bring the train's interior design back from the seventies.

I opened my shoulder bag and pulled out the mystery book I brought with me. I reached up and turned on the little light above the window. I was wholly engrossed in my book when I heard a voice ask if the seat next to me was taken. "Nope," I replied.

A wizard in a crisp navy suit was gripping my seat and the one across. The smell of alcohol still lingered on his breath. He sat down in the seat next to me. "I don't want to puke all over this four-thousand-dollar suit."

I looked up from my book. "This is my first time on a train, too."

"Oh, it's not that!" He said as he pulled out a flask from his suit coat and took a swig. "Oh, crap! Who finished off my whiskey?" he shouted belligerently.

"I don't know," I replied as I frantically looked for an escape route.

He smiled, showing off his pearly whites as he conjured up a bottle of whiskey and dumped it into the flask. He downed the entire container before returning to his tirade of how unfair his life was. Somebody loves his liquor. "If the stupid dragon hadn't broken his wing, I wouldn't be riding this outdated piece of crap! My company was too cheap to lend me another dragon. Can you believe that Acme Electronics had their head wizard take a crummy train to an international business meeting?"

"No," I answered, giving a sympathetic but fake nod. I really couldn't care less about this guy's business trip. I wish I had brought a pair of headphones. "So, where's a nice, young lady like you going?"

"I'm going to work at Urbana College of Magic,"

"Oh! You know what they say about UCM?" He didn't wait for my answer. "They say it's haunted by a ghost!" He made some lame spooky noises. "You better be careful there! You know how dangerous ghosts are!"

"It depends on the ghost."

"Right!" He raised a skeptical eyebrow. "Hey, would you like a drink?" he asked.

I was about to object when he said a magic spell and conjured up two Long Island drinks in his hands. "No, thank you!" I said.

"Fine by me!" he replied. My mouth dropped in shock as he downed both drinks in less than five minutes. Then he picked up his cell phone and began talking loudly about various business deals.

I went back to my book and tried to read it, but I was thinking about the haunting at UCM. Was it haunted, or was this the rambling of a drunk? If it were haunted, was that what Eddie had warned me about? The ghosts I knew were all very friendly. Maybe everything would have made some sense if Eddie had told me that he went to UCM.

About an hour later, I heard a timid voice ask if the seat facing us was taken. I looked up to see a red-headed vampire, barely in her twenties, holding a tiny, sleeping baby in her arms. She was pointing to the seat facing us. "All the other seats are taken."

There were other seats available, but once I read the vampire's mind, I realized that the Welkies on the train were shunning her. "Sure!"

Just as she sat down, the baby woke up and began to

wail loudly. "Shh, shh, little one!" she said in a soothing voice.

The wizard hung up his phone. "Oh, come on!" he shouted. He looked at me with an annoyed look in his bleary eyes. "I can't believe you let this bloodsucking hag sit with us! What is the world coming to when vampires sit with Welkies?"

My mouth dropped in shock as the vampire turned away. I could see the tears filling her eyes. Once I read her mind, I realized she didn't even know this man from Adam. Great! A bigot and a drunk! I turned to the wizard as a surge of righteous indignation rose in me. "Two things, buddy! Number one: I am not an enchantress. Number two: you are very rude to this woman!"

He scoffed at me, breathing the sour alcoholic smell in my face. "She's just a vampire. They don't even have feelings!"

This conceited racist was ticking me off. I stood up in my seat and flagged down the elf that was collecting the other passengers' tickets. "Conductor, sir! This man is very drunk and has insulted my friend here! Could you have him removed from his seat?"

It took the old elf only a few minutes to remove the

protesting, wasted wizard. Looks can be deceiving because the elf exhibited a hidden strength in extracting the troublemaker. When he came back to us, he said that he was a retired Marine in the Urbanan army. I turned to the vampire. "I'm so sorry, miss! There was no call for that!"

She wiped away the tears with the sleeve of her free hand. "It's alright! I'm used to it!" she replied.

"Used to what?" I asked.

She reached into a light blue diaper bag and pulled out a bottle full of blood for the crying baby. As soon as the blood touched his lips, he was content. "Welkies in Urbana detest any member of the undead. They think that we are filthy creatures who have no right to live!"

"If it makes you feel any better, I'm not like that. I like the undead. My boyfriend's a vampire. Here, I have a picture of him." I reached under my seat and pulled out my laptop bag. Unzipping the front pocket, it took a few moments to produce the photograph I took on Lisa's birthday last month. "That's my brother, Robin, on the right, and that's Eddie, on the left. We've been dating for about five months."

"You love him, don't you?"

"Yeah!" I said, blushing. I smiled as I put back the picture, and then I glanced at the baby in his tough, little overalls and green shirt. "How old is he?" I asked.

"Five months."

"He's so cute. What's his name?"

"Armand."

"Is he your first?"

The vampire smiled at me as she put away the bottle. Little Armand was full and happy. "Yes, he is, and he's a good baby, too. We were just visiting Grandma and Grandpa!" She reached out to shake my hand. "My name is Josette, miss!"

I shook her hand vigorously. "Shelly!" I introduced myself.

"Would you mind holding Armand while I use the restroom?"

"Not at all! I would love to."

"Thank you so much!"

Josette handed me the little one and slipped out of her seat. I cradled the baby in my arms and looked at him. "You are such a little cutie," I told him. He giggled and cooed. I wondered what a baby vampire thought. I began to laugh once I started to read his mind. Armand was thinking, "She's looking at me! I'm the focus of attention now! As it should be." He was enjoying watching the world revolve around him. Unfortunately, Urbanan Welkies didn't come to the same conclusion.

Eddie and I ever got married and had kids, what would they look like? *Whoa, Shelly!* I told myself. *Let's not be thinking about that right now.* If I mentioned kids to my boyfriend, I probably would scare him half to death. It was too soon in our relationship to be thinking about little Eddies and little Shellys running around.

When Josette came back, she flopped in her seat. We had about another thirty minutes before the train arrived at its final destination. I offered to watch Armand while she got some sleep. I entertained the baby vampire with his little, soft green toy bat.

"Next stop Merlin Boulevard!" The loud bellow of the train

whistle nearly pierced my ears as well as Armand's ears as he began to wail. He didn't like loud noises, and he was teething. No wonder the little guy was so fussy. Josette woke up and took him as she profusely thanked me for watching him.

Once the train came to a stop, we got off the train and said our goodbyes. I watched as Josette ran into the arms of a tall, burly vampire. After giving his wife a passionate kiss, he took his son from Josette and kissed him on the forehead. I watched the happy vampire family walk away, and I suddenly felt alone in this strange, new place. I missed Eddie. Swallowing the lump in my throat, I looked around the Grand Central Station look-alike. I hate being lost, and I knew nobody in Urbana.

"Miss Anderson?"

I turned my head to see a Winged One whom I estimated to be in his late sixties sitting in the driver's seat of a wagon pulled by a silver unicorn with a snow-white mane. Now, if you have never seen a Winged One, the only thing I can compare them to is an angel. They are humanoid in appearance, but the one thing that makes them different from humans is their enormous three-to-six-foot-long wings, which help them fly over thousands of miles. In his dark, golden hands, he held a sign that read: Michelle Anderson. Urbana College of Magic.

"Yes," I said to him, "that's me. Are you here to pick me up?"

He nodded. He flapped his long, peacock-blue wings and flew off the wagon. "President Blackstone wants you back on campus before curfew," he said with an accent sounding as though he stepped out of the pages of a Rudyard Kipling novel.

I glanced at my watch. It was only nine-thirty. "What time's curfew?"

"Eleven-your bags must be ready to be picked up." I followed him to the baggage carousel. With little effort, he lifted my bags into the wagon. I have heard Winged Ones' strength increases as they age. He flew up to the driver's seat, and I climbed beside him. "Allow me to introduce myself, Miss Anderson," he said as soon as we were on the well-lit road. "My name is Rajah Garuda, and I am the college's janitor. I'm at your service, Miss Anderson." He handed me a manila folder. "Here is a packet with your faculty ID card and a map of the campus, along with important information about the various buildings."

"Thank you," I said. There was nothing more to say that would have added substance to the conversation. So, I sat back and wrapped my arms around myself. Mrs. Yougha had told me the nights can get very cold in Urbana, and I was glad that I had remembered to put on my jacket before I left Zephyr. I looked out at the dark outline of trees casting strange shadows against the beam of street lights lining the roadway. As the wagon climbed up a steep hill, the campus of Urbana College of Magic illuminated the hilltop like a diamond in a dark mine.

We arrived at the ten-foot rod iron gates, and Rajah had to punch in a security code for the gates to open. He pointed to two five-story buildings as the unicorn took the wagon onto the golden brick road. I resisted the urge to sing a line from The *Wizard of Oz* because Rajah was about to give a quick visual tour. "Over there are the dormitories. One is for the male students, and the other is for the female students. They're pretty full during the summer, but now they are empty." The next building he showed me was Wizard Hall. Every class took place in this building. "The library is on the right!"

The library wasn't as impressive as the rest of the buildings, at least not on the outside. With the help of the streetlights sprinkled across the campus, the old, two-story building's red bricks were turning an unattractive shade of green from the mildew taking up residence along the sides. My hopes weren't held too high for the library's interior.

The wagon stopped in front of a two-story colonial blue apartment complex. "The women live on the first floor, and the men live on the second floor. The college has a stringent no-overnight-visitors policy," Rajah explained.

I nodded. I could stand two weeks of this. The Winged One helped me take my bags inside the lobby, where a young wizard in his thirties sat behind a large, chipped oak desk reading the morning paper. The once bright green carpet dating back a couple of hundred centuries certainly did not brighten up the dinginess of the place. The wallpaper reminded me of peat moss mixed with milk curds. I was sure there had been an intention of a design, but unfortunately, it portrayed a stunning image of fruit rings floating in a sea of soy sauce. *Lisa would go ballistic if she saw this,* I thought to myself.

"Adam, this is Shelly Anderson, the new librarian," Rajah said to the Welkie as he signed his name, with his left hand, in a three-ring binder.

Adam put down his paper and handed me a key. "You will be staying in Room 13, Miss Anderson. It's down the hall, second to last room on your left."

I thanked Rajah for his help, and I watched him get on the elevator marked Men. Wishing that I could grow a third arm, I managed to grab my shoulder bag, purse, and bags and rolled them down the hall. I reached the last room on the left and inserted my key into the lock. After realizing that my key wasn't working because I was at the wrong door, I noticed the door I was unsuccessfully unlocking had a rusty, empty plaque. My fingers had left imprints in the layer of dust on the knob. I must have been the first person to touch this door in years. Suddenly, I heard what I thought was some movement on the other side. Curiosity got the better of me, and I knelt to peer under the door. I could barely see past the dust. I gave up and went to the right room. Probably someone was cleaning in that room but in the dark?

I finally unlocked the door to Apartment Thirteen and immediately felt a rush of claustrophobia. The entire room consisted of two bunk beds with lilac bedspreads, one cheap black dresser, and a matching desk. Motel Six rooms rivaled the tiny one here. Did they design them with gnomes in mind? Sitting on the bottom bunk was a pretty elf in her mid-twenties. She immediately set her closed laptop aside and got up to greet me.

"Sorry, I took the bottom bunk," she apologized as she tucked back a piece of wavy, honey-colored hair behind one of her pointed ears. The huge, coke bottle glasses took away the beauty from her indigo blue eyes. Elves are just like humans, except for their pointed ears. "I'm Harriet Legolas, your roommate."

"Shelly Anderson. I'm the temporary librarian for the college," I said as I shook her outstretched hand. "I don't mind sleeping on the top bunk. I did it all the time in college."

The elf pointed her fingers and said, "Open empty

drawers!" To my amazement, the three bottom dresser drawers flew open. Usually, elves don't possess any kind of magic, and Harriet saw the shocked look on my face. "I'm half-elf, half-Welkie," she explained.

"Oh," I answered with a sheepish grin. I began to unpack my things and put them in the bottom drawers of the ugly dresser. The charger for my cell phone tumbled out of the towel, reminding me to call Eddie. I turned to my new roommate. "Do you mind if I make a couple of phone calls? I promised my boyfriend. I would call him when I got in."

"Not at all," Harriet said with a smile. "Just make sure you do it before curfew, or Professor Telle will have a huge hissy fit."

"Curfew must be pretty strict here," I said as I fished around in my purse for my cell phone. I knew it was a big mistake buying a purse that was about the size of Utah, as Eddie so kindly pointed out. I yanked the phone with a triumphant, sweeping gesture.

"Yeah, it gets worse during the school year. If you are caught up after curfew, you'll get at least twenty demerits."

That's ridiculous, I thought to myself. Do these people

have a life other than making their underlings' lives miserable?

"Is the demerit system only for the students?"

Harriet nodded. "Yeah, but the administration comes down pretty hard on us employees as well."

"Do they fire us?" I asked with mocking sincerity.

Harriet barely glanced up from her laptop when she spoke. "More than that! They strive to ruin our lives by giving us bad references. Sometimes they push you so hard you have to commit yourself."

The way she said it made me wonder if she was serious or just pulling my leg in some bizarre initiation ceremony that the college put on. This place was getting weirder by the minute, and I needed some solid answers. "You're joking, right?"

"You know why you're the new librarian here?"

I shook my head. "I was told the librarian up and quit without giving any notice."

"Actually," Harriet began as she glanced around the room as if she were sweeping for bugs, "there is a rumor around the campus that the former librarian went crazy. That's why she 'quit without notice.'" She used her fingers to place imaginary quotation marks around the last three words. "She 'claimed' to hear voices and said items in the library moved without any apparent magic."

I thought for a moment and then remembered my conversation with the wasted wizard on the train. "It sounds like she might have seen a ghost."

My roommate scoffed at me. "Are you serious? There is no such thing as ghosts."

"Well, actually, I have encountered some ghosts myself. Most of the time, they are just lonely and want someone to talk to."

"Oh!" Harriet replied skeptically. "I read in the *Journal of Conspiracy Theories* that ghosts are supposed to enjoy sucking the life from their victims, but of course, that's not true since they don't exist."

Great, I had a roommate who didn't believe in ghosts but believed every word of the supermarket tabloids. Did everyone in Urbana dislike the undead? I grabbed my cell phone and headed out into the hall when Harriet stopped me.

"You said you had a boyfriend. What's his name?"

"Eddie," I replied. "Here, let me show you a picture of him." I got the photograph out of my laptop bag and handed it to her.

"He's cute."

"I certainly think so."

"He looks so much like you, with his cute, deep blue eyes and his crew-cut brown hair. I love guys in crew cuts."

Eddie and I look nothing alike. Then I realized who she was talking about. "Oh, that's my brother, Robin." I sat on the bed next to her and pointed to the other guy in the picture. "That's my boyfriend, Eddie."

"Oh," she said as if I'd deflated her enthusiasm. "He's a vampire?"

I nodded.

"And you're okay with that? I mean, don't they suck the blood from humans?"

I shook my head. "Only the crazy ones! Vampires only drink bottled animal blood. If vampires drink human blood, they will go completely nuts and start killing people. Blood for vampires is more like an energy boost."

"What kind of animal does Eddie drink?"

"Oh, Eddie doesn't drink blood. He's a vegetarian."

"Really? Why?"

"Blood allergy. He gets sick whenever he drinks blood."

Harriet smiled and handed the picture back to me. "So, how long have you been dating him?"

"About five months."

"Wow! So, your brother doesn't have a problem with you dating a vampire?"

"No, Robin and Eddie are good friends, and my dad really likes Eddie too."

"That's the difference between your family and mine. If my father found out I was dating a vampire, he would kill him and then disown me for dating him in the first place."

"You're kidding, right?" I asked, not believing my ears. "You would be disowned for dating a vampire?"

She nodded as if it was common practice. "It's the Welkie way. I don't mind being around vampires and werewolves." She winked at me. "I'm more of a rebel."

I smiled hesitantly. It was going to take me a while to get used to all the cultural taboos and rules here in Urbana. "Well, if you don't mind, I'm going to step outside for a minute or so."

I walked into the hall and sat down on the torn carpet. When I dialed Dad's cell phone, I was directly transferred to his voicemail. That meant the diner was still open, and Eddie was still at work. After I left Dad a quick message, I called Eddie on his cell but was sent to voicemail. I smiled as I heard him say, "This is Eddie Van Helsing. I can't come to the phone right now. Please leave your name and number, and I'll get back to you as soon as I can. Thanks."

"Hey, Eddie, it's Shelly. I just wanted to let you know I got to the college safely." I glanced at my watch. It was almost eleven. "I can't talk long. It's almost time for the curfew to begin. Hope you had a good day at work. I'll talk to you sometime tomorrow night. Love you." I hung up, realizing what I had just said. "Wow!" I said under my breath. I just told Eddie I love him, and it wasn't just my loneliness talking.

Chapter Four
Something Stinks in the Town of Urbana

The incredibly loud wailing jolted me out of deep sleep. It took me a few minutes to realize I wasn't dreaming. I peered over the side of the bunk to find Harriet curled up under the bedding, gently breathing. "Harriet," I whispered to see if she was awake. No answer. Who was making that heart-wrenching cry?

Well, lying in bed wasn't going to do one bit of good. As quietly as I could manage, I crawled to the foot of the bed. The plastic-coated mattress creaked loudly as I carefully and quietly descended the wooden ladder. Once I made it safely to the ground, I unzipped my purse, muffling the sound as quietly as I could manage. After rummaging around, I found what I was looking for. I checked the batteries in the handheld flashlight. Good thing they hadn't run out yet. I listened for a moment or two for the crying, which had stopped suddenly as my eyes got accustomed to the dark dorm room. The mysterious wailing started up again. I looked over at Harriet. How could anyone sleep through that noise?

Maybe it's the law enforcement blood in me. With my ex-cop dad and my brother in the Zephyr police department, I can't resist a good mystery. I opened the door to the hall, which was just as dark as the dorm room. I hadn't bothered to check my portable alarm clock. It must be at least three o'clock in the morning. A very chilly air caused me to shiver in my pajamas and bare feet. I turned on my flashlight and swept the bright beam up and down the hallway. Nothing. At least the crying stopped. I was about to go back inside when I saw something move.

"Who's there?" I called softly as my breath appeared in front of me as if I were standing outside in the dead of winter. I turned my flashlight back on and almost jumped out of my skin. A young woman in a lovely blue dress was heading towards me. "Hey, were you the one crying?" I called out to her.

Another cold, harsh wind blew past me, and I shivered violently. My flashlight fell to the floor with a huge BANG, and as luck would have it, the light went out. I picked it up and attempted to turn it on. I smacked it against my palm a couple of times before a thin beam of light came to life. The strange woman walked in front of me. She moved very briskly towards the end of the hall to the weird door I had seen when I first arrived on campus. I tried to follow her with the beam, but it flickered and went out. When I hit the end of the flashlight into the palm of my hand, it came back on. Mental note: Buy new batteries in the morning. I shined the beam up and down the hall, but I was the only one there. Where did she go? There was nothing else I could do, and I went back to bed.

I jolted out of bed at seven-thirty in the morning to the annoying beep, beep of my alarm clock. I showered and put on a blue sweater and beige dress pants to go with my brown sandals. Grabbing a frosted pastry Harriet offered me, I headed out the door to meet President Blackstone in the lobby. I finished my breakfast just in the nick of time.

"Ah, Miss Anderson," Merrill Blackstone said as he got up from the green and yellow plaid couch, smoothing the wrinkles out of his charcoal gray double-breasted suit. The tall, very handsome (for someone in their sixties) wizard sauntered up to me. His white and black wingtip shoes clicked on the pink marble floor. "I'm glad to see that you are on time."

I smiled up at him as he shook my hand vigorously. "It's good to meet you, sir," I said. I noticed the strange emblem patch over the left breast pocket of his suit. It was in the shape of your standard shield with a black unicorn stabbing a griffin with its sharp horn over a blood-red background.

"Ah," the president said as he puffed his chest in pride. "I see you're admiring the Blackstone family crest." He pointed to the unicorn. "As you know, unicorns are furious beasts, and the rare black ones can kill your average griffin. The black unicorn symbolizes my family's strength and power throughout the ages."

"And the griffin?"

He raised a clenched fist. "To show our enemies, we'll destroy them once and for all!"

Alrighty then! Time to change to a less awkward subject. "Well, I'm very excited about working here."

President Blackstone came out of his take-over-the-world trance and gave me a movie star smile as he handed me a skinny folder. "Here is a list of relevant information about your job here. "Come along, Miss Anderson, I shall give you a tour of the library." He turned smartly on his heel and strode out the lobby doors with me following close behind. As we walked down the cobblestone sidewalk, the buildings reflected a sharp glare of the morning sun. "What kind of brick is the building made of?" I asked as I shielded my eyes with the back of my hand.

Blackstone smiled proudly. "When Urbana College of Magic was founded a hundred years ago, my great-grandfather ordered all the buildings to be made out of sparkle bricks so the college could be seen over thousands of miles away as a light for Welkies everywhere."

I could have sworn Blackstone's head of salt-and-pepper

hair was swelling a bit, but I'm proud to say that I calmly kept my mouth shut. "So, the college must be pretty influential here in town."

"Yes, UCM helped found the town. Many famous Welkies have graduated from here. Lord Marvin Tolkien is the founder of Tolkien Investment Firm and the third richest man in the Eastern Hemisphere! I graduated with him, as well as Georgia McMagic, the very successful actress."

"Does UCM only accept Welkies as students?"

"Exclusively. Ah, here we are!" Blackstone made a sweeping gesture toward the library building, nearly knocking me down. "Built a year after the college opened," he replied with an air of grandeur. He reached into one of his pockets and pulled out two sets of keys. He unlocked the huge cherry, French doors of the library and dropped the second set into my hands. "Now enough chit-chat. These are the keys to the library. Since it is during summer break, the library will not be open to the public. You can come in at any time to shelve books, order materials for next year, and do some general cleaning to get ready for the school year. Allow me to give you a quick tour of the library."

I gasped in amazement as the President ushered me in. The big cherry desk was equipped with the best and most expensive computer, the Magic Keyboard XP, and a high-end, high-quality printer. Even the Zephyr Public Library didn't have a red microsuede swivel chair! A spiral staircase led up to the horseshoe and opened the balcony to separate the two-story building. The entire building was lined with books, both old and new, reaching up to the ceiling. The cathedral ceiling was a masterpiece unto itself with paintings that no doubt told the heroic accomplishments of Welkies across the centuries. I wanted to study the artwork, but Blackstone distracted me with his bright, annoying smile.

"If you need to call me for anything, Miss Anderson, my office extension number is 248. Cheerio!" He called back as he strolled out the door.

I was alone in this gorgeous library. "Wow!" I said breathlessly as I leaned back in the beautiful cushy chair. When I first begin work at any new job, I like to know my way around the place. After setting the folder on the desk, I got up and wandered around the library. Fortunately, the college used the Mannical

Classification System (or MCS as we librarians like to call it.) If

you are familiar with the Dewey Decimal System, the MCS is a

breeze to learn. "What kind of books does an all-Welkie school

allow their students to read?" I asked myself as I grabbed the

first book under the Science section. *The Dragon Whisperer:*

Caring for and Feeding Your Dragon by Glenda Bruja, who,

according to the book jacket, "lives on a small farm in Pedestria

with her husband and five children." Interesting. I put back the

book and looked at one with a blue and green cover by the

talented wizard, A. T. Cauldron. *Potions for Beginners* had

recipes for turning princes into frogs, turning them back again,

putting a whole kingdom to sleep, possessing inanimate objects,

and even a couple of love potions.

I went to the next section of books under the subject of

Magical Technology. There were books on the do-it-yourself

wand and amulet repairing (which were outdated because

modern-day Welkies rarely use wands anymore), crystal ball

troubleshooting, and my personal favorite, *Broomriding for*

Dummies which had little cartoons throughout the book.

The next group of books I looked at was categorized as Social Sciences. The first book I looked at was titled *The Evil of Vampires* by none other than Merrill Blackstone. I began to flip through the first few pages thinking that it would be kind of funny to mention it tonight when I called Eddie. I instantly felt sick to my stomach when I read the first paragraph: "Would you let a vampire watch your children for even a few seconds? I would rather trust a hungry manticore to babysit any child of mine. Vampires are unfit to exist in society because they only want to suck the blood from the living." I slammed the book shut and leaned against the bookcase. Even though Bruce disapproved of Eddie and me as a couple, he would never be this vehement. This was a brutal, racist attack. I couldn't believe that anyone would want to publish this crap. I flipped open to the title page. That made sense: a small press company in Urbana owned exclusively by Welkies. All the vampires I knew were decent people, especially Eddie. Even the Welkies in Zephyr got along with the undead. For example, a vampire and a wizard were law partners in downtown Zephyr. Hoping this was the only anti-vampire book, I looked at the next books. The next book, written by President Blackstone himself, *Vampires: The New World Order*, was another acid tirade on how vampires are taking over the world by blood and brutality. President Blackstone had never met a vampire to realize how wrong his philosophy was.

I couldn't bring myself to even read the jacket covers of books on how to effectively kill a werewolf, various degrees of exorcism, and also one on what to do if your loved one has been turned into a vampire. Of course, the main gist of this lovely book was "to disown the family member to avoid any more embarrassment to the family." I thought it was odd that not one of the books had one good thing to say about the undead. Heck, I could write an entire book about a day in the life of a vampire and show this twisted world what they were really like.

I took an ancient green leather-bound book off the next bookcase. I glanced at the title, *A Study in Genie Servitude* by William R. Copperfield. This slightly less offensive work told the reader how to place a genie in servitude to the Welkie race. To enslave a genie, one only had to put a tablespoon of his blood in a secret compartment of a bottle handmade by the master. After buying a genie on the slave market, the Welkie marks the genie as his own with a branding iron of his family crest. According to Copperfield, "The inferior genie can't question his master's or mistress' order because he is incapable of disobedience. If he resists, the master is allowed to beat him into absolute servitude." I shook my head in disgust at this blatant, second display of bigotry. If one still had enslaved a genie, which I hoped not, maybe it could be freed. I carefully flipped to the index at the back of the book to see if there was any loophole. Bingo! I found the loophole. When I got to the right page, I found out that a genie's freedom can only happen if the secret compartment in the bottle is broken and the blood (which is perfectly preserved) is spilled. I never encountered a genie before, but the very idea of enslaving them made my stomach churn.

I had enough of looking at these disgusting books, and I sat back down at the main desk. For the first time, I noticed this year's student handbook sitting on the counter. *Where did that come from? It wasn't here before.* I glanced around thinking maybe President Blackstone or the janitor, Rajah, had dropped it off when my back was turned. But I was the only person in the building. "Creepy," I muttered as I began to flip through the poorly bound handbook. "This is interesting," I said when I came to the rules and regulations chapter. "Under no circumstances can students bring vampire lizards onto campus. Immediate expulsion will occur if one is found in a student's possession." What's a vampire lizard? And why can't a student have one on campus?

I reached under the desk and turned on the CPU. When the screen changed from black to bright blue, a message flashed across the screen, telling me I needed a password to gain access to the computer. "Oh, crap! I don't know any passwords." For the first time, I looked through the thin folder that Blackstone had given me. Flipping through the only two pages in the entire folder, the only information I had was the library's bank account information but no passwords for the computer. I picked up the phone and dialed President Blackstone's extension.

"President Blackstone, here!" answered a pompous voice.

Even though I didn't care for the president's politics, I was civil to him. "Yes, President Blackstone, this is Shelly Anderson, the new librarian," I said as I cradled the phone between my ear and shoulder.

"Yes, I know. Is there a problem that I can help you with?"

"I just need the password and username to log onto the library's computer."

"Well, I don't like to discuss passwords over the phone. I'll be over in a few minutes."

"Just tell me the password, sir. I won't say it aloud."

"Oh, all right!" He said in a defeated sigh.

I listened as I typed in the password and username and hit enter with one smooth stroke. "I got it, sir. Thanks," I said as I hung up the phone.

The wallpaper on the desktop showed a picture of President Blackstone staring up at me with a cheesy, movie star smile. I resisted the urge to puke and decided to explore some of the computer programs. Anything to get President Blackstone's face off the screen. I decided to click on a folder labeled, Students.

Once the program opened up, I remembered what Dad had told me. I wondered if I could dig up any dirt on Eddie. I did a keyword search on "Van Helsing, Eddie." No results. I tried the words "Eddie Van Helsing," "Van Helsing," and "Eddie." Each time was the same result. Absolutely nothing! That was weird. Why couldn't I find anything about Eddie? Maybe Dad read it wrong on Eddie's resume. I knew, for a fact, that he wouldn't have lied, especially to his employer.

Then I decided to do a web search on vampire lizards. According to an online encyclopedia, vampire lizards "are rare, endangered creatures that carry the vampire gene. Like most vampire animals, these lizards' bite paralyzes their prey, allowing the reptiles to drink their victim's blood. One bite from these extremely dangerous reptiles will turn anyone into a vampire." Oh, that made sense on why vampires only can turn others into fellow vampires through blood transfusions. Biting someone would render the victim helpless.

"Okay, Shelly, you've been lazy for long enough!" I reprimanded myself. I needed to get to work. Upon opening the top desk drawer, I found a list of books that I needed to order for the upcoming fall semester. Then I began the long process of ordering books. The first thing I did was open up a folder on the desktop marked "textbooks." Four more folders popped up with various names such as "undergrad, grad, faculty, and general. I chose "undergrad" and double-clicked on the "potions" file. After reading through the list of wanted books, I logged onto the designated website and began to process my order.

"What the?" I said aloud. The computer screen was telling me my bank account had insufficient funds. I triple-checked my order and came up with the same answer each time: insufficient funds.

Time to check out another source. I dialed one of the numbers on the list of information from the folder.

"Urbana Banking and Trust," chirped a very cheerful voice. "We keep your money safe. You can bank on it. Brittney speaking. How may I help you?"

Okay. There is cheerful, and then there is super-cheerful. Brittney seemed like the latter. "Hello, my name is Michelle Anderson, and I work at the library at Urbana College of Magic. I was ordering some materials, and there seems to be a problem with my bank account."

"What kind of problem?"

"It says that I have insufficient funds."

"Can you tell me your account number?"

I rattled off the number and answered a couple more security questions. The lady put me on hold for a few moments while I listened to tortuous polka music. Finally, Chirpy came back on and told me what she found. "A thousand dollars in the hole?" I asked her as soon as I recovered from the shock. "How is that possible?"

"Perhaps you overspent."

"No, my order only came to $380.00."

"Let's see," Chirpy said as she began to type away at her keyboard. "Okay, the campus library made an electronic transfer and withdrew a thousand dollars."

"Odd. What day was that?"

"Thursday of last week."

That made no sense. The last librarian had quit two

months ago, and from what I knew, no one else had been working at the library. "Just out of curiosity, how many accounts does the university library have with your bank?"

"Five."

"Is it possible that the money was transferred to an account?"

"No, sorry."

"Thank you for your time," I said and hung up the phone. What was going on? I decided to call President Blackstone. He would know what was going on. "Hello, President Blackstone?" I said once he picked up the phone.

"Yes?"

"It's Miss Anderson."

"Who?"

"Shelly Anderson, the temporary librarian here," I added helpfully.

"Oh!" he said as memory dawned on him. "What can I do for you?"

"There seems to be a problem with the library's funds," I explained what I found.

"Don't worry your pretty little head about it," he replied in a nonchalant tone. "It's nothing, I assure you."

"A thousand dollars is missing." *Does he not understand what I am saying?* I thought to myself. *Am I speaking in Klingon?*

"Perhaps you read it wrong."

"Uh, no! Someone took a thousand dollars from the library's budget."

"You're probably under a lot of stress with this new job and all. I think it's safe to assume that your math isn't up to speed." I was about to point out that the figure was what I had received from the bank, but he cut me off. "I strongly suggest double-checking your work. Oh, I'm so sorry, Miss Anderson, but I have to let you go. I have a call on the other line. As I said before, don't worry about a thing. Good day." He quickly hung up, not letting me utter a single syllable of good-bye.

I grunted in anger. Money is missing, and President Blackstone thinks that it's no big deal. "'You're probably under a lot of stress with this new job and all,'" I parroted the wizard's words with an exaggerated, high-pitched voice. "'Your math isn't up to speed. I strongly suggest double-checking your work.'"

Three hours later, I rubbed my eyes. They were sore from staring at the computer screen. I glanced back at page three of the long book list. Five more pages to go. I decided to get up and stretch my legs for a few minutes. Maybe get a drink of water and use the restroom.

I was in the middle of drinking the precious water at the fountain when I heard footsteps. I slowly let go of the fountain release and listened intently. They were coming from the balcony. "President Blackstone? Rajah?"

Nothing. Who was in the library? I dove under a table filled with cookbooks and then crawled on my hands and knees to the main desk. I slowly peeked over the top of the desk, feeling pretty silly. Spy work was not my forte..

There she was, shelving books on the second floor. Her long blue dress swished back and forth as she waltzed across the hardwood floor. Unfortunately, the only thing I could see was the back of her long, wavy black hair. "Hello?" I called out to her.

She didn't seem to hear me. So, I grabbed the edge of the desk and pulled myself up. When I looked up at the balcony, she was gone. "Hello? Hello?" I called, louder each time. "Is anybody out there?" I was only answered by an eerie silence. This place was getting weirder by the second. "Holy crap!" I said once I realized the time. The dining hall was closing in a half hour! I put the computer in sleep mode and ran to the dining hall, locking up the library as I left. Whoever was in the library couldn't come in again.

"Shelly! Shelly! Over here!"

I quickly turned around, nearly spilling my glass of water and a plate of food off the tray I was holding. I muscled my way through the crowd of elves, fairies, and Welkies returning their empty dishes to the booth where Harriet was sitting at a nearby table. "Hi, Harriet! Thanks for saving me a seat."

Harriet rolled back the sleeve of her purple smock to look at her watch. "The dining hall is about to close. You got here just in time."

I nodded. "I know. I lost track of time." I took a couple of bites of my cheeseburger and a sip of my water. "I am starving and sleepy."

"Why? Did you not sleep well last night?"

I shook my head. "I woke up in the middle of the night 'cause someone was crying."

"It wasn't me," Harriet replied. "'Cause I slept like a log."

"I know. I went to investigate."

"And?"

"I saw a young woman in a blue dress walking down the hall. When I tried to talk to her, she didn't seem to hear me. And then she suddenly vanished. Get this! I saw her again in the library. The same thing happened when I tried to approach her."

Harriet looked at me as if I had forgotten to take my medications. "Right? And nobody else heard or saw her?"

"I guess not."

"Shelly, are you feeling okay? I barely know you, and I don't want to sound crass." She hesitated as if she wanted to form her next few words very carefully. "But maybe you just imagined the whole thing."

"Maybe, you're right. I did have a late night," I replied as I dipped a fry in the ketchup. Harriet was right. The woman must have been a figment of my imagination. When I was little, Dad had always told me not to let my imagination run wild. But what if there were no logical explanation for what I saw?

The rest of the day was uneventful. President Blackstone replenished the diminished funds. I didn't even care where the money had come from. After spending close to three hours staring at a computer screen, I was ready to call it a day. When I closed the library at seven-thirty, I stopped by the little restaurant on campus and ordered a to-go meal of grilled chicken salad and a chocolate milkshake to compensate for that one thousand-calorie burger I had for lunch.

Harriet was talking on her cell phone when I walked into the room. For some strange reason, she immediately changed subjects with the person on the other line. I shrugged, not knowing why she did that. As if I were going to listen in on her conservation. I grabbed my cell phone and dinner and walked to the end of the hall.

As soon as I dialed Eddie's number, I opened up the little packet of light Caesar dressing and poured it over my salad. The phone rang a couple of times before he answered. "Hi, Eddie!" I said, leaning against the wall.

"Hey, babe! How was your first day at work?"

"Okay," I said as I bit down on a forkful of lettuce, cucumbers, and grilled chicken, "Sorry, I'm eating dinner as I'm talking."

"Well, do you want me to call you back in a few minutes?"

I shook my head. "No, I want to talk to you now."

"I feel special."

I smiled. "Well, you are."

I could almost see Eddie smiling back at me. I realized how much I missed being with him and sighed. "I miss you."

"I miss you, too, Shell."

"So, how have you been holding up?" I took a couple of sips of my milkshake. It wasn't as good as the milkshakes Eddie makes at the diner.

"Fine, we played poker last night."

"Did you win?"

"Nah, Strider won this time. That guy has some serious gambling issues. What about you? How was your trip?"

"Okay, I got to hold a baby vampire on the train ride. He was so adorable!"

"Oh, boy! Don't get any ideas, babe," he said with a laugh.

From the tone of his voice, I knew he was joking. Eddie liked kids. "So, I'm staying in a dorm room here on campus," I told him all about the strict policy at the college. "I feel like I'm in a maximum-security prison, but you would know that because you went here, didn't you?"

"Uh, yeah, I guess so."

"How come you didn't tell me this before?"

"It must have slipped my mind, Shelly."

Right, I thought to myself, *as if you forgot*. I wasn't going to push my luck. "I wanted to see if I could dig up any dirt on you."

"You didn't, did you?" Eddie suddenly became very

apprehensive. "Did you?"

"Calm down, Eddie. I couldn't find any trace of your records."

I heard a huge sigh of relief on the other end of the phone. "It was probably some kind of computer glitch."

"Or someone purposely erased your school records?"

He laughed nervously. "Right! It's all some kind of big conspiracy."

"That's what my roommate said when I told her about the weird thing I saw!" I told him all about the mystery woman in the hall and the library.

Eddie was quiet for a while after I had finished my tale. I wished I knew what he was thinking, but my telepathy with vampires only works if they are in the same room as me. "Shelly," he said hesitantly as if he was avoiding the possibility of incurring my wrath, "don't take this the wrong way. I think you might have been seeing things. I mean, you have been stressed out lately."

My shoulders tensed. "I'm not stressed, and I didn't imagine seeing her," I informed my boyfriend through clenched teeth.

"Whoa, Shelly! Calm down! Let's change the subject."

"Did you know how prejudiced this town is?"

"Doesn't surprise me."

"Were you working uncover here?"

There was a long silence. "Look, Shell, I've got another call. It's important."

Liar, I thought but didn't say it to him. "I'm going to let you go, Eddie," I said between yawns. Staring at a computer screen for five hours can make anyone sleepy. "I'm going to bed early."

"You do sound like you're tired. Talk to you later, babe."

"Bye, Eddie." I slowly closed my flip phone and finished up the last remains of my salad and milkshake. I was mulling over the way he had acted on the phone. I knew little about his past. I did know he used to be a spy, a bounty hunter, and a racecar driver. Beyond that, I barely knew him. He was usually open with me whenever I asked him anything. Why the sudden change?

I gathered my junk and walked back to my room. Harriet was reading a romance novel in bed when I went inside. "How was the rest of your day?" I asked her.

She placed the book on her stomach and looked up at me. "Pretty boring! One of the professors burnt himself with an exploding spell, and one of the cooks broke his leg after taking a spill on the waxed kitchen floor. So, the clinic was pretty busy. Who would have thought being a school nurse during summer break would be so exciting?"

I shrugged. "Were you talking to your boyfriend when I first came in? I didn't mean to interrupt you on the phone earlier."

"No, I don't have a boyfriend. I was talking to my Uncle Sid. He was the one who set me up with this job as a clinical nurse."

I remembered Harriet's comment about Robin. "Hey, are you looking for someone?"

"Why? Is your brother available?"

"I could ask him."

"Would you? I mean, Robin—that's his name, right?" I nodded, and she continued, "He is really cute."

"I'll mention the next time I talk to him." I yawned again and stretched my arms over my head. I did my nightly routine, made the long trek up Mount Bunk Bed, and said good night to Harriet, who was gracious enough to turn out the overhead light for me. I quickly fell asleep to the soft tapping of the keys on her computer laptop.

Chapter Five

President Blackstone is a Creepy Man

As an observer only, I find myself amidst a large crowd of college-age Welkies inside a dismal warehouse. Bright and harsh spotlights are focused on an amateur four-posted boxing ring.

"I've got 500 druci on Abbott!" someone screams in my ear.

"Put me down for 650 on Dreyson!" A young wizard thrusts a roll of bills into someone's waiting hand.

I am shoved to the front of the screaming mob. My eyes finally see what the excitement is about. Two humanoid genies are circling each other in the pit. The purple-skinned one is almost seven feet tall, as is his green-skinned companion. His long hair pulled back into a tight ponytail, is crusted with purple blood. His muscular body is naked except for a pair of shorts and marked with thousands of scars. On both of his upper arms are ancient, burnt images of the Blackstone family crest. Under each brand is a barely glowing tattoo of a butterfly emerging from a cocoon.

"Abbott," a much younger Blackstone hisses at him angrily from outside the ring. "What are you waiting for? Kill him!"

"I can't, master. He is too powerful."

"I have 3,000 druci betting on you! Do not make me lose this fight! Now, kill him!"

The crowd is whipped into a frenzy, screaming, "Kill! Kill! Kill!" The genie slowly nods and morphs into a giant saber-tooth tiger taking up the entire ring. Before the other genie has time to defend himself, Abbott rips him in two with one swipe of an enormous claw.

I don't know what awakened me: the disturbing dream or the loud wailing coming from outside my room. This time I was determined to see what was troubling the mystery woman, I quietly crawled out of bed with the flashlight I had expertly placed right next to my pillow. I glanced over at the sleeping Harriet. She needed to know that I didn't hear things. "Harriet? Harriet?" I hissed as I shook her shoulder.

Harriet rolled over to face me. "What's going on? Why are you waking me up at this ungodly hour?" she asked in a groggy voice.

"Can't you hear that?" I raised my voice over the crying.

"Hear what?" she asked. "And why are you yelling?"

"Someone is crying in the hall!"

She got out of bed and looked at me as if I were crazy. "Shelly, nobody is crying."

I grabbed her hand and yanked her near the door. "I'm serious, Harriet. Someone is crying out in the hall." I opened the door. "Look if you don't believe me."

We both peered down the darkened hall, looking both left and right for any signs of life. Finally, Harriet looked at me. "Are you pulling my leg?" she demanded in an irritated voice.

I glanced up and down the hall. If we were the only people around, then who was making that noise? "No, someone is crying," I insisted. "I'm not hearing things," I said it more to convince myself than Harriet.

"Well, I don't hear anything. I'm going back to bed." She closed the door, leaving me alone in the hall with the crying only I was apparently hearing.

I drew in a sharp breath. I guess I was going to have to figure this one out all by myself. If I woke up anyone else, they would have to ship me off on the next train to Psychoville. The sobbing soon became labored breathing as if someone was gasping for air. I listened intently to learn where the weird sound was coming from. As soon as I turned on the flashlight, I followed it until I arrived in front of the room with the locked door. With the aid of the dimming beam of light (I had forgotten to replace the batteries today), I noticed the doorknob hadn't been touched since I had attempted to open it earlier. I pressed my ear against the door, hearing footsteps inside. I crouched down to take a peek under the door after I tried to unlock it. Someone was definitely there, but I had no idea if they were male or female. "Hello?" I called. "Is someone in there?"

The pacing immediately ceased, and I received silence for my answer.

"I'm Shelly from next door. I heard some crying. Is everything all right in there?"

"Who are you talking to, Miss Anderson?"

I looked up to see President Blackstone standing only inches away from me. "Uh, President Blackstone, I think my ID card slipped under the door when I dropped it." It took me only a few moments to come up with a plausible lie. It was more believable than if the crazy librarian was hearing things and talking to her imaginary bunny friend, Harvey. The wizard gave me a disbelieving look. So, I made up another lie on the spot. "I have insomnia. I decided to get some water out of the vending machine. Can't have soda 'cause it keeps me up at night."

He flashed me a charming smile. "Well, it's late, and you should get back to bed," he admonished me in a tone that was supposed to come across playfully but came out very creepy.

I turned and rushed into my room, slamming the door behind me. *God,* I thought, *Harriet must be a really sound sleeper because I would have woken myself with all that loud noise.* Men, unless they were on the maintenance crew, weren't allowed on the women's floor. So what was President Blackstone doing there at three o'clock in the morning?

I lay in bed as the dream kept playing over and over again in my head. Genie death fights! Who would commit such a heinous act? Why was President Blackstone in my dream? None of it made any sense. Maybe, it was something I had read earlier. As hard as I tried, I couldn't fall back asleep.

I decided to spend my day at the library shelving books on the second floor. Balancing the pile of six books on my hip, I casually glanced at the beautiful stained mahogany railing that ran around the edge of the balcony. That's when I noticed the two different shades of mahogany on the third section of the railing. I set the books down on the floor and went for a closer inspection. Most of the handrails had been there for well over a hundred years covered with scratches and indents, but I could see a darker shade of paint like Lady Macbeth attempting to wash the blood off her hands.

I began slowly backing up as I got the feeling that something terrible had happened in this library many years ago. WHAM! I had forgotten that there was a bookcase behind me. An old-looking book tumbled from the top shelf and onto the floor. I bent down to pick up the old business textbook and began gently flipping through the yellowed, stiff pages when I noticed a folded piece of brown paper. Something told me I should see what it was. Carefully I peeled apart the paper and began glancing over the scribbled notes about stocks and economics. This was Eddie's handwriting! What was it doing in a book about business? In the bottom right-hand corner was a circle drawn around a note that read, "Tell Fern about Merrill." Eddie always did that to remind himself of important things. Who was Fern? His ex? I refolded the paper and gently stuffed it into the pocket of my blouse.

"Miss Anderson!"

President Blackstone's voice jumped me. The old book in my hands clattered to the floor with a loud THUD! I bent down to pick up the book with the now broken spine, all the while my rear end facing the staircase,

"Nice bu—book!"

I instantly straightened myself up and whirled around to face my new supervisor standing at the head of the stairs. "President Blackstone!" I exclaimed as I smoothed out the imaginary wrinkles in my pants. He was showing up at the most inopportune moment, and was he trying to hit on me? "What are you doing here?"

"Please call me 'Merrill!' I was wondering if you would like to have lunch with me in my office. There's a great view of the city from my window."

"No, thank you." I picked up the stack of books from the floor and began to shelve them.

Suddenly, he grabbed my elbow hard. "Michelle, I insist."

I told him that I preferred "Shelly" to "Michelle." What was this creep trying to pull? A sexual harassment case? "Sir, it would be inappropriate!" I jerked myself free of him.

"No one has to know!" He reached for me again.

"Don't touch me again!" I warned him. Then I had an idea. I tossed the pile of books at Blackstone and ran to the other end of the balcony. My heart pounded in my chest as Blackstone began to head towards me. This was not a good situation. I was alone with a creep with no one to help me.

"Mr. Blackstone, I repaired that leaky pipe in the men's room!"

I gave a massive sigh of relief as Rajah flew up to the balcony. He stood between me and Blackstone, who suddenly replaced his angry frown with a false smile. "Is there anything else I can help you with, sir?" the Winged One asked.

"No!" Blackstone snapped. He spun on his heel and tramped down the stairs in a fuming manner. Rajah and I listened as he slammed the library doors behind him, rattling the books so hard that they nearly fell off the shelves.

Rajah turned to face me. He must have sensed the fear written all over my face. As he bent down to help me gather up the books I had thrown at the wizard, he said. "Be careful, Miss Anderson!"

"Yes, I know these are old books. They slipped out of my hands."

"No! I meant—." He lowered his voice. "Be careful around

Mr. Blackstone. Even though he is a good employer, he has no morals when he is around women." He handed me a pile of books. "Let me know if he gives you any kind of trouble."

I nodded my thanks to him and began to put the books away. Rajah flew back down to the first floor and left me all alone. It took me a few minutes to stop shaking from the massive scare I had received. Sure, I had faced gargoyles and huge spider demons before, but Eddie had always been there right beside me. I had no idea what I should do about Blackstone hitting on me. Right then and there, I decided I would call Eddie tonight and ask for his advice.

Nothing else happened for the rest of the day. Blackstone avoided my gaze whenever I saw him at lunch, dinner, and walking to my room. I didn't mention the incident in the library to Harriet when I met her for meals. What would I say? It would be my word against Blackstone's.

I stopped by the little convenience store on campus and picked up batteries for my flashlight. If I were going to do some unexpected investigating, I was going to be ready this time.

Then I decided to check my email with my laptop when I got

back to my room. Harriet had gone out for the evening with a

couple of friends. At least that's what her note said. I suspected

that she was out shopping for the latest edition of the *World

Weekly News.* I liked Harriet, eccentricities and all.

All that my email inbox had to offer me were three

coupons from a bookstore and a cute joke about a panda

walking into a bar, the latter Eddie had sent me. He always

knows how to bring a smile to my face. While I was online, I

decided to see if Blackstone had any trouble with the law, but my

search proved fruitless. I grabbed my cell phone and dialed

Robin's cell phone.

He answered on the second ring, "Y'ello?"

"Robin, I've got a favor to ask of you," I said.

"What are you up to now, Shelly?" my brother demanded.

"Could you see if a wizard by the name of Merrill

Blackstone has any kind of criminal record?"

"Why?"

"I'm doing some private research," I lied. There was no

way on earth, I was going to tell my brother about Blackstone's advances towards me. The last thing I needed was Robin playing vigilante/overprotective brother.

"I can't, Shelly. I'm not at the station right now."

"Oh, come on, Robin! This is the first time I've ever asked you for a favor."

"More like the hundredth!"

I chose to ignore my brother's snide remark. "Look, I'll set you up with my roommate."

"Is she Jennifer Aniston hot or Cindy Crawford hot?"

"More like Jennifer Aniston, I guess. Her name's Harriet."

"Will you send me a picture?"

"One condition: you get that info for me."

I heard my brother rummage around his apartment for a pencil and paper. "What's the guy's name?"

"Merrill Blackstone." I spelled it out for him. "Next-Day the info to me if you find anything. I brought my digital camera with me, and I'll email you a picture of Harriet."

"Fine by me. How's your new job?"

"Good," I replied, "the school is fairly strict, but I'm only going to be working here for two weeks, so I can stand it."

"That's cool. Look, I've got to go. Roger, Eddie, Strider, and I are going to a movie right now. Talk to you later, Shelly. Bye!"

"Bye, Robin! Thanks for everything." I hung up the phone. That meant I would have to call Eddie after eight to tell him what happened. I relaxed and read the murder mystery I had checked out from the library.

Once I finished the book, I checked my watch. It was just after seven. I climbed off my bed and pulled out a lined notebook and pack of colored pencils. I could spend the rest of my time working on the templates for the invitations. Once I was back on top of the bed, I pulled out the piece of paper with the list of design ideas Lisa had given me from the notebook. Since the wedding colors were silver and royal blue, I began crossing out a few of the ideas that wouldn't match the color scheme. Royal blue hearts and silver rose petals might look great for Valentine's Day but not for a winter wedding.

The next idea was a chapel amid a meadow of

wildflowers. It would take at least three hours just to complete the template. I skipped over the ideas that had little children and the cute dog and cat playing dress-up. If Dad and Amelia were in their twenties, then maybe it would be all right. I gave a great sigh. This was going to take a long time, and I didn't have a single brilliant idea for the invitation.

I called my dad on his cell. "Hey, Dad," I said after he answered.

"Oh! Hello, Shelly, how's your week been?"

"Okay! Nothing too exciting!" I lied. I hate lying to my father. He is very protective of me, and the last thing I wanted was for him to worry about my safety. "Are you busy?"

"No, Amelia and I are at lunch. What's up?"

"I need some ideas about wedding invitations."

Dad laughed. "I don't know if I should be the one giving you advice. You should ask the bride."

"It's your wedding, too, Dad!"

"Here, let me put you on speakerphone."

"Hi, Shelly!" Amelia's voice came over the phone. "You're

having trouble designing the invitations?"

"Yeah," I replied, "no ideas are coming to me right now." I rolled over onto my back and put my feet up against the wall. "What do you want the invitations to say about your love for each other?

Dad sighed. "Well, I think Amelia has always thought of me as her knight in shining armor."

"Timothy!"

I could almost see my stepmom-to-be blushing. "How about a knight carrying his princess bride to his dragon-guarded castle?" I suggested as I began a simple sketch of an armor-clad knight carrying a princess upon a unicorn.

"Ooh, that sounds like a beautiful idea. You can put morning glories and baby's breath along the path to the castle."

"I can do that. What do you want the invites to say?"

"Oh, I've got that," Amelia replied. "Mr. Timothy Michael Anderson and Mrs. Amelia Jean Cross request the honor of your presence to celebrate their love at the Chapel of Love on December 10th at 3:00 pm."

I jotted it down as she spoke. Tears of happiness began to

stain the paper. My dad was going to be happy again. Even though I missed my mom every day, I was so glad that Dad was no longer going to be a widower. *Better stop getting emotional, Shelly,* I told myself. *Or the paper will be floating in a mini-ocean.* I wiped away the tears with the sleeve of my shirt. After getting another piece of paper, I worked on another sketch. "So, is the diner busy?" I asked as I sketched the unicorn.

"Not really," Dad said. I overheard someone yell for him in the background. "Shelly, I've got to go. I'll let you chat with Amelia." He must have turned the speakerphone off.

"How is your job going?" Amelia asked me.

"All right. It's a little weird. They're fairly strict here, but the work is interesting. I have never worked in an academic setting." Amelia's grandmother was the head librarian at an Ivy League college, so she somewhat understands the way of the librarian. I wanted to tell her what happened to me, but I certainly didn't want to worry her. With the help of my karate skills, I knew I could take care of myself. "So, where's Dad taking you for the honeymoon?"

"He won't tell me."

"It's probably going to be somewhere very romantic," I guessed as I finally finished with the first sketch.

"Speaking of romance, how are things between you and Eddie? I heard that he saw you off at the train station."

"Okay, I guess!" I began darkening the lines of the drawing. "Since I got the job here, he's been super protective of me, but he wouldn't tell me why. I don't get it. Eddie's my first boyfriend, and I'm new to this relationship thing. Is there something wrong I don't know about? What do you think, Amelia?"

"Well, I believe that Eddie cares a lot about you. He wants you to be careful."

"But why?"

"I don't know, Shelly. That's something you and Eddie have to talk about."

I was about to ask Amelia how I should approach this situation when I received an incoming call. "Got to go, Amelia. Eddie's calling me on the other line. Bye." I hung up and picked up the other line. "Hi, Eddie!" I said.

"Shelly, why did you ask Robin to do a criminal check on Merrill Blackstone?" Eddie asked.

"'Why, hello, Shelly!'" I said. "'How are you doing?' 'Fine, Eddie. Thanks for asking.'"

"Very funny," Eddie replied in a somewhat irritated tone.

"Why are you asking about Blackstone? Was he an old-school chum of yours?"

"Hardly." The vampire's voice suddenly had an acerbic tone to it. "What did he do to you?"

I told him about the meeting in the hall last night and in the library. "I mean, he was creepy." I gently touched the small bruise that had started forming on my elbow, where Blackstone had grabbed me. "All I wanted to know is whether or not this guy has a criminal record."

"Shelly, I want you to be careful around Blackstone. He's a dangerous man!"

"How do you know?"

"Because he hurt someone very close to me a long time ago."

"Was it someone named Fern?"

There was a hesitant silence.

"Eddie," I spoke up as I remembered the strange note. "I found this note you wrote." I pulled it out of my pocket. Not wanting to rip it apart, I slowly unfolded it. "It says, 'Tell Fern about Merrill.' Who's Fern?"

The other phone suddenly clattered to the ground, nearly bursting my eardrums. I listened for Eddie to pick up the phone, and when he did, I heard a distinctive click. "Eddie? Eddie? Hello? Are you still on the phone? Can you hear me now?" I glanced at the LCD screen: Call Ended 02:47:18. He had hung up on me! For what reason? Perhaps when he dropped the phone, it accidentally shut off. I decided to call him again and was immediately sent to his voicemail. "Eddie, I don't know what happened, but call me back when you can. Talk to you later."

Chapter Six
My Roommate Becomes My Prime Suspect

Nothing too exciting to write home about happened in the next few days. I hadn't seen the mystery woman again. Perhaps I had imagined the whole thing. Then something strange and all too exciting finally happened. I had gotten up early one morning to do some investigating of my own. As soon as I let myself into the library, locking the door behind me (the last thing I needed was Blackstone creeping up behind me), I started up the computer, thinking about my boyfriend.

Eddie still hadn't returned my last call, and he's pretty good about stuff like that. Late last night, I had concluded that something awful had happened here at the college, and Eddie was somehow involved. I went on the popular search engine,

Findit.com, and typed in the words, "Urbana College of Magic history." After sifting through a hundred sites, and that was just the first page, I let out an exasperated sigh. Can't the Internet be more organized? There had to be more specific words that I could use in my search. Just when I was about to give up on the tenth page, I noticed the title of the fifth link: Urbana College of Magic Librarian Dies Accidentally. I opened the link and read the paragraph-long article from forty years ago. "The body of a young Urbana College of Magic student was found in the campus library yesterday morning. Police are ruling her death as accidental. More information on the woman's identity will be released once her family is notified." Strange! I wondered who this woman was and how she died. I printed out a copy of the article.

First, I decided to get on with my real job and opened the library doors. After loading up a cart with a pile of books from the new book section, I headed back to the computer. After logging into the library's cataloging program, I began switching the location from new books to the regular stacks. This program was about five years out of date. As I read the introduction to the program, the user was recommended to save every few entries. Most of the new books had been at the library for over twenty years and were seriously outdated. What Welkie still uses brooms as a form of transportation? No one I knew. I was about halfway through the status changes when the computer screen went completely black.

"No!" I nearly screamed after I realized I had forgotten entirely to save my work. I scrambled for the reset button and nearly jammed it into the CPU, cursing to myself for my stupidity. Once the computer came on, a purple message ran across the blank screen, saying: "Stay Away! Beware!" Where did that come from? I tried to move the mouse. When that didn't work, I tried random typing on the keyboard, but still, the same message was running continuously across the screen. Something with strong magical abilities was lurking around the library, and it was no Welkie.

I saw Harriet walk right past me at the front desk. She apparently didn't see me when I waved to her. My roommate walked past the medical and magical herbal section of books.

She made her way to the back of the library, opened the door leading to the basement, and slipped inside. She was definitely up to something.

Grabbing the small flashlight that was kept in one of the drawers, I left the desk and followed her. I opened the door to discover a set of long dark stairs. Harriet had a flashlight with her because I could see the beam bobbing up and down in the darkness. Slowly and carefully, I felt my way down the stairs, trying not to make a sound without killing myself or blowing my cover. I dove behind a padded water heater, praying I wouldn't encounter any member of the rodent family.

After deciding the racket she heard was the water heater, my roommate walked to the far left corner of the basement. A cloud of dust flew up from the floor all around her when she knelt in front of a stack of three cardboard boxes. She set the flashlight on the ground so that I could see the lettering on the boxes. *Why is she looking at old yearbooks?* I thought to myself from my hiding place. *Why is she so covert about it?* She opened up the first box and began flipping through the first book. After finding nothing of interest, she set it down beside her and looked through another one. After a few minutes, she had accumulated quite a pile of books.

My hand brushed against something furry, and I had to bite my tongue to stop the shriek erupting from my mouth. Once I realized I hadn't touched a mouse, but only a piece of insulation, I breathed a much too loud sigh of relief. Just as Harriet turned her head, I flattened myself on the dusty cellar floor, giving me a perpendicular view from under the water heater.

"Who's down here?" Harriet demanded as she waved her flashlight beam around, barely missing me. She pulled something from the pocket of her smock, but I couldn't quite see what it was because I was too busy concentrating on the huge cockroach that was about two inches from my nose.

Leave! I mentally hissed at the insect. I could've swatted it away but wisely decided against the idea. Not exactly a big fan of cockroaches, then again, who is? And knowing me, I would have blown my cover. Then what lame explanation could I give Harriet? That I was looking for leaks in the water heater? James Bond always made it look so easy.

To my relief, the bug scampered away, frightened by the sudden ringing of Harriet's pager. The elf picked up her flashlight off the ground and headed up the stairs, closing the door behind her with a loud click. I was now left all alone in the damp, smelly basement.

I came out of my hiding place and, with the help of my flashlight, made my way to the pile of books. Tucking my flashlight under my chin, I opened the first book in the collection. Except for the fact that UCM's yearbook, *The Oracle*, was in top condition, I found nothing unusual at all. What was Harriet looking for here? After searching through every book in the pile, the only thing I noticed was dust and a couple of squashed bugs. With my flashlight in one hand, I pulled out the next book in the box. Glancing at the year on the cover, I made a quick mental calculation.

This yearbook is from forty years ago, around the same time as that student's death, and when Eddie was turned into a vampire, I realized. As I flipped through the first few pages, I noticed that one page had been carefully cut out near the end of the master graduates' pictures. Strange, why would the school accept a yearbook with missing pages? I carefully searched through the other pages, making sure no other pages had been cut out. Once I got to the pictures of the undergraduates, I noticed the very last page of the juniors had been cut the same precise way. Turning to the index, I ran my fingers down the T-V section. "Valiente, Darren, Van Faustus, Jerald—What?" I stared at the two thin strips of White-Out that covered the next two names. Using my thumb as a bookmark, I flipped through the rest of the index to see if any other names had been crossed out. There weren't any.

I managed to scrape away the cover-up on the first name. "Van Helsing. Edgar Van Helsing. 'Edgar?'" I began to giggle. Was that Eddie's full name? I always thought it was something like Edward or Edwin, but definitely not Edgar.

I was about to scratch away the first name when I heard heavy, hideous wheezing coming from behind me. I slowly turned around and let out a terrifying scream at the creature in front of me. It was an enormous floating dark purple head with a mess of tentacles, each with an eye on the end. Amid this menacing head-thing was a mammoth-sized eye and a gaping mouth with thousands of bloodstained teeth. Right above the inner eye was the Blackstone family crest. The thing's long, black tongue darted out at me. "Oh, crap!" I screamed as I scrambled to my feet. A blue streak of light shot out from the middle eye, barely missing me and vaporizing the boxes into a pile of ash. I sprinted up the stairs so fast the Flash would have eaten my dust. I slammed the door behind me, and I leaned against it attempting to control my labored breathing. What was that thing down there, and where did it come from?

After lunch, I went up to President Blackstone's office. I needed to tell him about what happened in the library. As I approached the President's office, I could hear two people shouting coming from behind the closed door. It was hard enough not to eavesdrop on the conversation. Anyone on campus could listen to them.

"I can't do this anymore for you!" a gruff voice said. "Someone will find out!"

"Oh, please! A genie with a conscience. That's new,"

Blackstone said in an arrogant voice.

"I did my job. Now, have someone free me!"

"You are free when I say you are free," snarled

Blackstone. "And no, you did not obey me. I told you to kill her,

not scare her."

"I will not kill for you again."

"You will do as I say, or shall I pour acid on your marks

again?"

"Someday, you will pay for your crimes."

Suddenly, Blackstone's dropped his voice into a low

whisper. "Nobody threatens a member of the Blackstone family!

Now go do what I told you to do, Abbott!"

After I gathered up enough courage to face the angry

wizard, I rapped on the frosted window of his office. "Come in!"

Blackstone bellowed in a strangely cheerful mood.

"It's Shelly Anderson!"

"Oh, come in!"

I opened the door and stepped inside the office that was

about the size of a hotel room. The faded orange walls were lined with framed certificates, letters of recommendation or appreciation, and various accomplishments. Boy, was this guy full of himself or what? Blackstone's huge black desk with gold trimmings took up about half of the room. A three-drawer metal filing cabinet sat on the desk's left side while a tall black bookcase filled with books on leadership and academic management was on the right side. The wizard got up from his expensive-looking red leather chair to greet me.

I looked around the room. "I thought I heard someone else in here with you."

Blackstone averted his eyes for only a moment. "Miss Anderson, you caught me."

"What do you mean?"

"One of my secret hobbies is ventriloquism. I was just practicing. Would you like to hear me?"

"Uh, sure?"

"Hello, Miss Anderson!" His horrible attempt at throwing his voice was like watching a badly dubbed foreign film. "So, what do you think?"

I paused, mulling over the proper response in my head.

"You've got potential," I finally replied.

He didn't catch the bald-faced lie. "Miss Anderson, I want to apologize for my attitude yesterday. It was very unprofessional of me!"

Yeah, and people in Hell want ice water. "Forget about it, sir!" I told the arrogant jerk. *I won't press charges just yet.* Then I told him about what happened in the library. I subtly omitted the part where I had followed Harriet down to the basement and replaced it with the lie that I smelled something strange coming from the basement. "I just wanted to let you know that a couple of pages had been cut out of a yearbook."

I must have said something wrong because Blackstone gave a nervous laugh. "Oh," he said as he stared at a bottle decorated with brilliantly colored flowers that were sitting on the filing cabinet, "the yearbook must have been that way when the school received it as a donation."

"Doesn't the school keep their copies of yearbooks?"

Blackstone's speech faltered a bit as he quickly changed the subject. "That thing you saw in the basement. It must have been your imagination! I have never heard of anything as you described."

I wanted to insist that I was not crazy, but then who would believe me? Suddenly, I remembered another thing I wanted to ask him about. "Sir, did an Edgar Van Helsing ever go here?"

Blackstone seemed to ponder awhile before answering. "Edgar Van Helsing? No, I have never heard of him. Why do you ask?"

"On the damaged yearbook, someone had taken White-Out to two of the names in the index. I was able to scratch one of them off, and that's the name I saw."

He glanced back at the bottle. "Like I said, I've never heard of the name."

What's so important about that bottle, I wondered. I decided to find out. "That's a beautiful bottle, sir."

"Oh, you like it?"

I nodded. Sure. Why not? "It's interesting."

"Well, it's been in my family for generations. One of my ancestors was an extremely wealthy glassblower and handmade it himself."

"Oh!" I automatically reached out to touch it, but Blackstone slapped my hand away, very hard.

"Don't touch, Miss Anderson! It's very fragile."

I was too shocked to say anything.

"Now, about that name! You must have read it wrong, Miss Anderson. But this has been a pleasant conversation. We must do it again sometime. Now, if you will excuse me, I have a critical phone call to make." He waved me off as if I were some kind of a lowly servant.

A few minutes later, I found myself back in the library. I walked over to the computer on my desk. Everything was working fine! Even the entries that I lost when the computer crashed were already in the program. "That's strange," I said aloud. "I never fixed the computer." Then I was taken aback the moment I saw the time for the last entry. It was done not more than two minutes ago! Did the computer crash, or had I imagined the whole thing?

I decided to check the basement to make sure I wasn't

completely losing my mind. After clicking on the lights, I descended the stairs expecting to be engulfed in smoke. No smoke, no burning boxes, and no disfigured monsters chasing after me! I stood in the middle of the basement with my hands on my hips. Even my water heater hiding place had been entirely undisturbed. It was as if no one had been in the basement for years, not a few minutes ago. "No, no, Shelly. You are not going crazy." I said in a failed attempt to reassure myself. "Someone or something is messing with you!" That's when I smelled a cleaning solution. Someone had done a great, but fast cleanup job of the hot mess. But who and why?

I trudged back upstairs and began putting away some books-anything to keep my mind somewhat sane. It was going to places that I didn't think it could go, like Crazyville. Maybe President Blackstone was right. I probably had imagined the monster attacking me. Then again, I don't believe that I could have come up with a creature that ugly. I was so lost in my thoughts that I barely saw the mystery woman standing beside me. For the first time, I caught a glimpse of her face. There was something familiar in her eyes that I couldn't quite place. *Who are you?* I wondered.

Leave me alone! The mental message was filled with an icy cold bitterness. She disappeared right through the bookcase.

I peered around the other side, but she was gone just like that. No trace of her anywhere. Then I realized something. I had just telecommunicated with her! She was a ghost. That explained why I was the only one who heard the sobbing. The minds of ghosts tend to wander frequently, and a telepath can read ghosts' minds, just as long as they are near the phantom. So the rumors around here were true! A ghost was haunting the library, but who was she and why was she so sad?

That night, I was once again all alone in my room. Harriet was out as usual. The other night I heard her come in well after ten o'clock. I had never thought of Harriet being a social butterfly, but then again, I'm a homebody myself. This would give me a perfect chance to call Eddie on his lunch break. I wanted to tell him what I had discovered. He usually has lunch between eight and nine, providing that the diner wasn't busy, and I knew that he would be outside having lunch on the picnic table behind the restaurant. "Hey, Babe!" he said the moment he picked up his phone.

"Hi, Eddie," I chirped.

"So, how was work today?"

"Guess what I discovered today!"

"What?"

"I know what your full name is," I replied in a sing-song voice.

Eddie laughed. "Really?"

"It's Edgar," I said with a giggle.

"It is," he confirmed. "How did you find that out?"

"In an old yearbook."

He let out a sigh. "Why do you think I go by 'Eddie'? I hate my full name!"

"Oh, come on. I think it's a great name. It sounds noble, refined, and—." I paused, trying to think of some other adjectives to describe the name.

"And dorky," the vampire replied. "Edgar was a popular name when I was born, but nobody uses it anymore. It's become obsolete. Please, don't ever call me 'Edgar.'"

"I'll try to remember that!" I replied.

"Other than that, how was the rest of your day?"

I told him about the weird things that had happened in the library and Blackstone's excuse. After assuring him that Blackstone didn't make any moves on me, I told him about the ghost. "She seems upset about something, but I don't think she wants to talk to me about it."

"Maybe she doesn't want to talk about her past."

Like you, I thought to myself, but I didn't say it. I knew little about the vampire's past, and he never liked to talk about it. To this day, I still don't know why I opened my big mouth at the next moment. "Eddie, who was Fern? Was she your old girlfriend?"

I heard the phone drop to the ground and listened to Eddie taking in short gasps of air. Then suddenly the phone went dead. This time it wasn't an accident. He had hung up on me for no reason!

I called him back, but all I got was his voicemail. "Eddie, is everything all right? If this 'Fern' was an old girlfriend, it doesn't matter to me. I don't care about your past relationships. I just want some answers, and I feel like you're not telling me everything. Please, call me back!" I closed my phone and gave a great big sigh. I loved Eddie so much, and I knew that he loved me too. Then why was he hiding secrets from me? What had happened to him at this school that was so terrible?

I needed to talk with someone whom I trusted. So the next call I made was to my best friend. "Hey, Lisa," I said when she picked up.

"Hi, Shelly!" Lisa replied. "How was your trip?"

"Good, I met this vampire with her new baby boy on the train. He was so cute!"

"I bet you thought about having kids with Eddie."

I smiled, "Well, the thought did cross my mind, but if I mentioned it to Eddie, he would probably freak out."

"I think you two would have beautiful children."

"Whoa there, Lisa! Let's take things one at a time. Eddie and I have to be married first."

"Do you think you guys will ever get married?"

I sighed wistfully. "I hope so. I would love to spend the rest of my life with Eddie, but can a relationship thrive on secrets?"

Even in high school, Lisa had lots of boyfriends. But ever since she came to Zephyr after a bad relationship, she's been taking a break from the dating scene.

"What do you mean?"

I told her everything that had happened to me in the last few days. "Eddie's just acting so weird lately. He didn't tell me he went to UCM, and now with this ghost that I keep seeing, he's acting weird."

"Do you think that the ghost might be his old girlfriend?"

"I don't know. I asked him, and he hung up on me!"

"I don't know Eddie as well as you do, Shelly."

"I wish he would just tell me what's going on. I hate being kept in the dark like this."

"I wonder if that note you found had something to do with a love triangle that Eddie was involved in."

"I don't know. Something about this place has been troubling me ever since I arrived. I believe that something terrible happened here, but nobody wants to talk about it."

"Have you asked the President of the college about this mystery lady?"

"No, I'm staying away from that creep!"

"Okay, so what about the janitor? Maybe he did something bad, and that's what the school is hiding."

I shook my head. "I don't think so, Lisa. I think that Rajah is covering up for Blackstone. He must be the one who cleaned up the mess."

"So, what's in it for Rajah?"

"Job security, maybe? It sounded like Rajah has been at UCM for years. Maybe he served jail time before he started working here."

"You know Fiona Littlehorn, the elfin reporter for the *Herald*?"

"Yeah, Robin trained with her husband, Airis."

"Well, she's going to be interviewing me tomorrow for a newspaper article. It's going to help boost up some clientele for the business. I bet she can find some articles about Rajah's past."

"That would be great! Call me tomorrow and let me know

what you find out. His full name is Rajah Garuda." I spelled it out for her. "And he is a Winged One."

"Got it," Lisa replied after she jotted it down. Finally, she asked a question out of the blue. "Did your Dad ever have a problem with you dating Eddie?"

"At first, yeah, but he got over that. Dad likes him. Eddie had just started working for Dad when I first met him. He is Dad's best worker. Why do you ask?"

Lisa sighed. "Remember you told me Dirk was hitting on me the first time I met him? Well, I want to date him, but I know my dad won't approve."

"I know your father doesn't like Eddie, but I think you should follow your heart. Dirk's a nice guy, although a bit annoying at times."

"He's a great musician. I love hearing him play his guitar. Shelly, Dirk is so hot! I can see why you're dating his brother! Okay, you can read vampires' minds. So, does Dirk like me?"

"Oh, yeah! He thinks you're hot, but he hasn't asked you out yet because I think he's afraid of Bruce."

"Yeah," Lisa replied with a sigh, "Dad doesn't think I should date a sexy vampire."

I smiled. The Van Helsing brothers are handsome. Of course, I'm dating the hotter one. I could tell in her voice that she wanted to date Dirk. Lisa flirts with Dirk every time I'm with them. Even Eddie has noticed it. "For one thing, Bruce can't tell you who to date and not to date. You're a grown woman, Lisa. Dirk has to ask you out. Look, I'll have Eddie talk to Dirk."

"Thanks, Shelly. You just made my night." I heard her give a great big yawn. "I'll call you with any info about that janitor."

I glanced at my watch. It was getting past my bedtime. "I'll let you go then. Bye, Lisa!"

"Bye, Shelly!"

As soon as my call ended, I dialed Eddie's cell phone and left a message telling him about Lisa's feelings toward his brother. As soon as I was done, I changed into my pajamas and crawled into bed. Great! I was playing detective and matchmaker. I hoped that everything would work out perfectly. There's nothing I hate more than a mystery.

Chapter Seven

Robin Sends Me Some Dirt on Blackstone

My mail came right before lunch. So I had a chance to flip through the full package Robin had sent me. I was a little bit concerned about the damaged seal when I opened my mailbox. Someone was breaking federal law by opening other people's mail, and I was positive that the college was not above the law. Nothing seemed to be missing from the package. What were they looking for? Drugs? Anthrax? One of those vampire lizards? It seemed to be just a pile of white paper.

Then I noticed the small penlight stuck at the bottom of the page. This was no ordinary penlight. If you turned it on, invisible ink would become visible under the pale purple light. Of course, you have to be in a dark room to read the words. Government agencies once used this particular type of ink and pen to transport confidential documents, but now more modern security devices are being used. *Good thinking, Robin,* I thought to myself as I hurried back to my room.

Once I locked myself in the bathroom, I knelt on the floor beside the toilet. I set the papers on the closed toilet lid and proceeded to sift through the information with the specialized light. "Wow!" I said quietly. "Blackstone is not exactly the man you want to bring home to meet the 'rents!"

Over the years, there were about a dozen harassment cases filed against the wizard by women he worked with and dated. But none of them ever went to court. Either the woman dropped the charges, or she died before the trial. I also noticed the women still alive had sudden increases in their bank accounts soon after the charges were dropped. It looked like Blackstone had paid them to keep their mouths shut, but then again, wouldn't the Urbana police have noticed this pattern? I rechecked the dates and realized that the dates were too scattered to make any sense at all. I wondered if Blackstone paid off the officers investigating the cases.

The next file nearly took the wind out of my sails.

Blackstone had a wife? Some poor soul married the creepy jerk?

Eww! Technically, Eva Spellman was his dead ex-wife. Eva left

Merrill after she decided he wasn't going to beat her anymore,

both physically and emotionally. During the divorce, she placed a

restraining order against him after he kicked in her door. Right

before the hearing, Eva "died under mysterious circumstances."

Her death was ruled a suicide.

Another odd thing about the women was one common

denominator: every single one of them had at one time or

another, worked at the campus library in one capacity or another.

Did Blackstone have a thing for librarians? "I know that we

librarians are the fulfillment of some men's fantasies, but this is

ridiculous!" A big piece of the puzzle hit me like a speeding train.

Blackstone had used these women to cover up something.

Robin had added another sheet of paper, a list of

Blackstone's finances. There were sporadic bits of evidence

showing the wizard was in thousands of dollars of debt every few

months. For example, he was $5,000 in the red one month, and then his debt was barely cleaned up. The reason soon became

apparent. On the first and third Friday of every month, he would

take money out of the library's budget and place it into his

personal bank account. Sneaky little devil! Who would look into

missing money from the library? The sports fund, yes, but not the

library.

I noticed something familiar about the dates when he

replaced the library budget. I compared them to the list of

girlfriends' harassment file dates. They were within a few weeks

of each other. I needed to do some more investigating and check

the newspaper archives. I jotted down all the dates on some

scrap paper and stuffed it into my pants pocket.

I checked my watch. My lunch hour was almost over! I

grabbed the papers and ran out of the bathroom and into the

bedroom. Where to put the papers? I decided to stuff them into

the bottom of my suitcase. Then I ran back to the library at full

speed.

I nearly ran headlong into Rajah, who was cleaning the

windows of the library. The bucket full of soapy, bubbly water spilled all over the marble floor. "Oh, I'm so sorry, Rajah!" I exclaimed as I helped set the bucket upright.

"It's all right, Miss Anderson!" the Winged One replied sadly as he picked up the sponge off the floor. "I'll go get a mop!"

"Well, let me at least help you!" I followed him to a nearby closet where he retrieved two mops. I took one from the old janitor and began to wipe up the wet floor. "I never got to thank you properly for helping me out with President Blackstone the other day."

"It was the least I could do. Mr. Blackstone is a bad man."

"How so?"

Rajah looked around as if someone was spying on him. "Mr. Blackstone likes to hurt women. He has done awful things to them."

I gave a non-committal nod. Just by reading the files Robin had sent, I knew that Blackstone was a pig. For some unknown reason, a voice that I did not recognize as my own inside my head said, *Ask him about the locked door.* "Rajah, there's a locked room at the end of the hall on the women's floor.

I heard someone moving around inside, but nobody seemed to be there. I've been wondering why it's locked!"

The janitor jumped up in fright. His wings shuddered violently at the mention of the locked door. "I don't know what you are talking about!" he replied nervously. He finished mopping the floor without another word and left the library in a hurry.

What did I say? All I did was ask him about the locked room. At last, I was left alone to do some detective work. I headed upstairs. The microfilm room was a small and very stuffy area with one machine and two bookcases taking up the entire city. After turning on the device, I headed to the first bookcase with my list in hand and pulled the box with the corresponding dates. I began to sift through the box for the first date. "You've got to be freaking kidding me!" I said aloud to no one in particular. Nothing, absolutely nothing! Oh, sure, there were the months before and after, but that particular month was missing. I triple-checked the box. Still, nothing turned up. "Okay, Shelly, this is a library," I reminded myself. "Things disappear all the time."

I gave up finding the first date and went on to the next one and the next one until I had gone through the entire list. The same thing every time. Every single newspaper article was missing. "Maybe they're misshelved." An hour passed, and I had gone through every single box three times. It was like those dates never existed. Blackstone had gotten rid of them to hide his crimes. The little weasel covered up his tracks pretty well, but not for long. This was going to be the first time he encountered a librarian with law enforcement blood running through her veins. Plus, I knew an alternative method of research.

I went back to my computer downstairs and logged onto the internet. After moments of searching, I found the Urbana Public Library's website and checked their hours. They closed at ten. "Perfect!" I said, rubbing my hands together. "I'll go there once I get off work." The library was a few minutes' walk from the campus. How convenient! I would have plenty of time to check out their newspaper archives.

I began rearranging a section of books when I saw my mystery lady standing beside me. She turned and gave me a genuine smile. As I opened my mouth to speak, she disappeared into the bookcase.

"Hey, wait!" I called after the ghost. "Don't leave! I want to talk to you! I know you're probably lonely because nobody believes in you, but I do! Don't be afraid!" Without warning, a big, two-inch book flew off the shelf at warp speed straight at me. I ducked way too slow and WHAM right in the nose! Once I removed my hands from my face, blood began spurting from my nose. Tipping my head back, I pinched my nostrils together and sprinted across the campus to the clinic.

The fairy sitting at the receptionist's desk took one look at my bloodstained blouse and asked in a sweet voice, "What is your emergency?"

"My nose is bleeding, profusely!" I replied.

"Okay," she replied in a cheery flight attendant voice, "just fill out this form, and a nurse will be right with you." She handed me a two-page form attached to a clipboard and went back to her work.

I sat down and tipped my head forward. This was great. How the heck was I supposed to fill out this two-page form without bleeding all over it? "Excuse me, do you have a tissue?" I asked the receptionist.

"Sorry, I don't have any!"

Super! The one time I come to the clinic, they don't have a single tissue! I grabbed one of the other forms and used it as a very primitive napkin. I glanced at the form after filling out the necessary information. Reason for visit? My nose bleeding like Niagara Falls.

Minutes later, I presented the complete form with minimal blood splatter to the receptionist. She took it from me and proceeded to enter the information into the computer. "I know this may not be important, but is there any chance of me seeing a nurse, like now?" I asked.

"Well, we're running late. I'm afraid that you are going to have to be patient."

I was about to protest when Harriet came around the corner. She gasped the minute she noticed the copy paper doing a pathetic job of stopping the nosebleed. "Shelly, what happened?"

"A book fell on me!"

"Quick, let me see!"

I followed her around the desk and into a puke-green room where she had me sit up on the examination table, which was a lovely shade of grimy mustard. The protective paper crinkled absurdly loud as I shifted to staunch the flow gushing from my nostrils. Nurse Harriet laboriously filled out the forms, while I waited, holding myself rigid to keep the stupid paper quiet. Harriet finally completed the paperwork, not seeming to notice the streams of blood oozing between my fingers and dropping loudly on the paper. Turning to me, she cheerily questioned, "So, what seems to be the problem?" I pushed aside a wave of irritation at being asked about my condition when it was so freaking obvious.

"Well, a book fell on my face, and now it's bleeding pretty badly if you haven't noticed." I inwardly kicked myself for attempting to set this dullard up with my brother.

"Oh. I see. Well, here's a tissue, and we'll start by taking your blood pressure."

"That sounds super." Just don't mind the pint of blood

dripping from my nose and saturating the paper on the chair. I transferred the copy paper to the tissue as a tourniquet for my nose.

After about ten minutes of having my temperature (98.6° Fahrenheit) and blood pressure (slightly elevated due to my irritation) taken, and making sure that everything, except for my nose, was A-Okay, Harriet pulled out some gauze from the supply cabinet above the sink and handed it to me. "This will help control the bleeding."

About time! I removed the sopping wet tissue and placed the gauze below my nose, pinching the bridge to constrict the blood flow, which had slowed down to an oozing pace. "Thanks!" I allowed the elf to look at the bloody damage. I nearly shrieked in pain as she applied pressure to my tender nose.

"Can you breathe through your nose?"

"Barely!"

She took out an X-ray pen and pointed it directly on my nose. These nifty pens give an immediate X-ray to medical professionals. "It looks like you slightly fractured your nose. I'll go get some magical green unicorn lotion. Your nose will be healed in no time." She hurried out of the room.

I stared at the wall chart of the human body with the muscular, skeletal, and cardiovascular systems. I was desperate because all the magazines were out of my reach, and the latest one was dated August of last year. Old magazines in a doctor's office? Shocker, I know. That's when I noticed a notepad on the nearby desk on top of what looked like a yellowed patient folder. Curiosity got the better of me, and I reached across the examination table and managed to grab the notepad.

I began to read through the writing on the lined paper. "'Forty years ago, a 20-year-old woman claimed that one of her fellow students physically assaulted her. I searched for the report, but it wasn't in the file. Possibly destroyed? Connected to murder?'" Why was Harriet looking at old patient records? I wondered if she was a nurse. She sure didn't act like one. Who had hurt this young woman? I was about to reach for the folder when I heard footsteps coming towards the door. I scrambled over to the table and placed the notepad right back where I had found it, just as the door opened.

Harriet gave me a quizzical look as I froze in place reaching halfway over the table. "Is everything all right?" she asked.

"Oh, I was just trying to get one of those magazines on the desk," I lied.

She definitely didn't buy it, but she said nothing. From her lab coat pocket, she pulled out a small tube about the size of a toothpaste tube. She unscrewed the cap and squeezed a small amount on the fingertips of my free hand. "Rub this all over your nose right now and again tonight. The magic in the lotion will repair the fracture by tomorrow." She gave me the bottle after I did as I was told. I could feel the cartilage in my nose, putting itself back together. I love magic.

"All right, Shelly, you're all set. See you tonight. Call us if you need anything."

"Thanks!" After I paid for the tube at the reception desk, I left the clinic and headed toward President Blackstone's office. After I had told him about fracturing my nose, he said I could go back to my room for the rest of the day. I took some aspirin for the splitting headache that was developing and went straight to

work. I didn't go back to my room.

Chapter Eight
I Learn Something New

I first noticed the genie following me the moment I left the campus. He trailed a few feet behind me all the way to the public library, even when I made a couple of misleading turns to shake him. Persistent bugger.

The brick two-story library took up almost an entire zip code. The inside of the austere building had polished black marble flooring and crimson red walls. The books in the mahogany bookcases seemed to be no less than fifty-years-old.

I walked up to the mahogany desk where a gray-haired enchantress in a high-collar navy blue dress was typing away on a computer. She looked at me over the rim of her glasses. "May I help you?"

I nodded. "Can you tell where your microfilm room is?"

"Right up those stairs!" she replied, pointing to a winding, marble staircase with a golden railing near the back of the building.

"Does it cost anything to print?"

"Twenty cents. The machine only takes coins, though. "

I reached in the bowels of my purse and pulled out a crumpled five-dollar bill. "Can you make change?"

She took my money and exchanged it for a handful of coins. "Remember, the library closes at ten."

It was only six o'clock. I thanked her and was halfway up the stairs when she called out to me. "Miss, your genie can't come in here!"

I turned around and spotted Abbott, who had just walked through the front door staring at me with his arms crossed. "Isn't this a public library?" I asked, surprised.

"Yes, but we don't allow his kind in here," she said snippily.

"But it's a public building, and anyone should be allowed in here."

"We maintain a high standard of decency."

"By treating someone like Abbott as if they were second-class citizens? That's not what a public library is supposed to be. People of all races should be able to come in and have access to information."

She was seething now. "Miss, you get that creature out of the building, or I shall call the police."

I hated doing this, but I really didn't want word to get back to Blackstone that I was here. Finally, I gave in, not willingly. "Abbott, will you wait outside for me?" I told him, hoping he would obey someone other than his master.

He nodded sharply and vanished in a cloud of purple smoke.

I walked upstairs and entered the microfilm room that was bathed in a sea of royal blue paint. There were five mahogany bookcases, in keeping with the motif of the library and three microfilm machines. I grabbed a velvet blue, high back chair, and winced from the screeching noise as I slid it across the marble floor to the microfilm machine of my choice. Then, I took out my list and began to pull the corresponding microfilm off the shelves.

This time I found every single date.

I fed the reel through the machine and rolled it forward until it landed on the article I was looking for. Trisha McSpell, the campus librarian, died after overdosing on prescription drugs. I recognized the name. She was the first librarian who had pressed harassment charges against Blackstone. Died a few weeks after the library budget was raided.

All of his girlfriends, it seemed, had "accidents" or died within a month after money went missing from the library. "Okay, that piece of the puzzle is solved, but what is he covering up?" I asked myself as I straightened my stack of copied articles. I was mulling over this conundrum when I spotted the librarian standing in the doorway with her arms crossed.

"Can I help you?" she asked.

I was about to say no, but then I remembered my strange dream. "Yeah, what do you know about genie fights?"

She gasped. "Those horrid things were thankfully outlawed here in Zephyr over one hundred years ago. Some of the more uncivilized Welkies decided that it would be fun and profitable to have their genies fight to the death." She shook her head in disgust. "Disdainful sport. But unfortunately, I have heard rumors of illegal fights within the city limits."

"By 'profitable,' do you mean gambling?"

"Oh, yes. I remember my brother, Tyler, telling me about one he went to where he lost several thousand dollars on a purple genie. But then, the next week, the genie won, and my brother doubled his winnings." She paused and looked at me. "Why do you ask?"

"I'm doing a report." All right, not a total lie but just a half-truth. I gathered up my things. "Well, all of this information should come in really handy for my paper. Thank you for everything," I told her and quickly left the library.

The genie was waiting for me at the bottom of the front steps. Jeez, this has got to stop! "Hey, Abbott! Why are you following me?"

He began to turn into a hideous creature. Then he stopped and stared at me while I stood my ground. "Why aren't you trembling in fear?"

"Because I know you don't want to hurt me."

He stared at me with his glowing eyes. "How can you be so certain?"

"Because of the conversation you had with Blackstone. You were only following orders."

He changed back into his normal, humanoid form. "You're right. I realize how different you are from others. You didn't fall for my master's charms."

"Well, he's kind of creepy, and I already have a boyfriend whom I'm pretty devoted to."

"You are also the first person I have seen in a long time who stood up for my kind."

"How can you work for that snake?" I asked. "He's a thief and possibly a murderer."

He snorted a derisive laugh. "Foolish mortal, you know nothing of genies. We have no choice but to obey them."

I was shocked. "Really?"

He sighed. "Yes, these things," he pointed to the two burn marks on his arms, "keep me forever enslaved to him."

I gasped. "How long have you been with the Blackstone

family?"

"I had just celebrated my 20,000th birthday when a slave trader sold me to Abram Blackstone over six hundred years ago. His handmade bottle containing his blood has kept me bound to this despicable family forever."

My mind flashed back to that book on genies. "Can't you just break the bottle?"

He gave another rueful laugh. "If I could, I would've been free a long time ago. The blood bond can only be broken when the bottle is broken, and the blood is spilled by a non-family member."

As we walked back to the campus, I learned a lot about genies that I never knew. Genies are immortal, nomadic people who live in another dimension. They're divided into four tribes: purple-skinned shapeshifters, blue-skinned elementals (power over earth, wind, fire, and water), red-skinned fortunates, and silver-skinned gemologists (can create precious stones out of anything.) The tattoos on their bodies represent their powers and glow bright when in use. But when enslaved, the brand marks slowly diminish the tattoos' glow.

When we arrived at the campus gates and were about to go our separate ways, I asked Abbott one last question. "If someone could free you, what would be the first thing you would do?"

"I would kill Master Blackstone," he said in a somber tone before disappearing in a cloud of smoke.

The dining hall had closed, so I spent another ten dollars at the campus restaurant getting a large vanilla iced coffee and a chicken stir-fry meal. As I sat all alone at a booth, I checked my messages. Lisa had called me back with both good news and bad news. The good news was that Dirk had asked her out, but the bad news was the information I had asked about. Rajah's crimes were three counts of shoplifting back when he was a much younger man. So, the old man hadn't done anything really bad, but it made me wonder what he was protecting Blackstone from? The other message was from Robin telling me how much he liked the picture of Harriet I had e-mailed him. He really wanted her phone number so that he could talk to her. No messages from Eddie. What was going on with him?

After dinner, I went outside in the fresh night air to call my boyfriend and sat down on the brick wall away from the general flow of traffic. He picked up on the third ring. "Y'ello?"

"Hey, Eddie!" I said.

"Hey, babe! How's it going?"

"I fractured my nose today."

"What did that maggot Blackstone do to you?"

"Nothing!" I replied, shocked at Eddie's harsh tone. "A book literally flew off the shelf and hit me in the nose. I'm okay. It's almost healed. I've been thinking about it, and I think someone's out to get me."

"Maybe the books don't like you," Eddie replied in a much more gentle voice, obviously sensing my shock. "Have you been handling them roughly, Michelle Anderson?"

I hate my full name, and Eddie knows it. He loves to tease me about it. Now I had ammo to shoot back at him. "Not funny, Edgar Van Helsing!" I playfully scolded him. I was about to mention what I learned when I heard a soft voice next to me say, "You know my brother?"

I looked over my shoulder to see the ghost sitting next to me on the wall. "Um, Eddie," I said. "I've got to let you go. Bye!" I quickly hung up on him and turned to face her. "Who are you?" I asked.

She gave me a sad smile. "Fern Van Helsing. Edgar Van Helsing is my brother!"

"What?" I said in complete shock. "That can't be right! Eddie doesn't have a sister." I looked at her closely. Gosh, maybe it was true. She did have Eddie's eyes and that same captivating smile. "That I know of."

"He's never mentioned me?" she protested.

"No, and neither has Dirk."

"Why?" she asked as she cupped her head in her hands.

I put an arm around her shoulders. "I don't know. Why don't you tell me what happened?"

Fern swallowed hard. "I was working on my bachelor's in library science here at the same time Eddie was training to become a vampire slayer like Dad. Our father was a famous

wizard who helped vanquish a vampire militia group."

"Wait a minute! The Van Helsings are vampire slayers?"

She nodded. Holy crap! No wonder Eddie never talked about his

past. A vampire slayer turned into the very thing he was hunting.

"Be careful of Merrill," Fern warned me. "He'll hurt you.

He's got a genie doing evil things for him. That creature that

scared you in the basement was really a genie! Merrill's very

evil."

"What do you mean?"

Fern began sobbing and slowly faded away. I was left all

alone with some of my questions, both answered and

unanswered. Eddie had never told me about Fern, but I gathered

from her conversation Merrill Blackstone had done something

horrible to her.

Chapter Nine
I Do Something Slightly Illegal

I slowly walked back to the dormitory and barely noticed the flashing lights of the campus security. Two centaurs were carrying a stretcher holding a covered body. I almost missed the green feather falling from the stretcher as I walked up to the small crowd of onlookers gathered near the lobby doors. "What happened?" I asked as I hurried up to Harriet, who was standing in the front row of the mob.

"Didn't you hear? Rajah Garuda committed suicide today in his apartment!" Harriet said in a low voice.

"But I just spoke to him this afternoon, and he seemed fine."

"Yeah, President Blackstone found him after he didn't show up for work."

"How did he die?"

"Shot in the right temple. At least, that's what the police were saying."

"Are the Urbana police investigating his death?"

Harriet shook her head. "No, the campus police take care of crimes that happen on campus. President Blackstone heads the investigations."

I nodded, but I didn't agree. My investigative mind began going into overdrive. It would have been difficult for Rajah to shoot himself in the back of the head. Did Blackstone suspect that Rajah was going to let me in on the wizard's scheme? Or had the janitor become a liability? I decided to take things into my own hands.

Later that night, after everyone was fast asleep, I slipped out of my dorm room with my flashlight in hand. I pulled down the hood of my sweatshirt to keep a low profile. I crept quietly past Adam, who was snoring away at the desk in the lobby. A cardboard replacement of him would have the same effect. Ah, tuition dollars at work! I hit the elevator button to the second floor and dashed at the moment the doors opened, completely unnoticed.

Accessing the coast was clear, I stepped off the elevator and glanced down the darkened hall. Now, which one was Rajah's room? I looked around, expecting to see the famous yellow tape across a door. Knowing Blackstone, he probably cleaned up the scene of the crime himself after he killed Rajah. Nah, he wouldn't kill the old janitor. Blackstone was the type of person who wouldn't get his hands dirty. He must have had Abbott do the dirty deed. It was the perfect crime. Blackstone would get off scot-free, and Abbott would never get a fair trial.

"Shelly?" a soft voice asked beside me.

I whirled around to face the owner. "Fern, you scared me!" I said in a low whisper. Of course, she was supposed to haunt people. "What are you doing here on the men's floor?"

She smiled at me. "I'm a ghost. I can go wherever I want. I could ask you the same question."

"The janitor supposedly committed suicide today, and I'm trying to find out what really happened."

"I'll show you to his apartment." She took my hand. It was

cold but not clammy to the touch. She led me down the hall to the fifth door. "Rajah has lived in this apartment for over fifty years. I saw Blackstone and that awful genie go in there. They started shouting, and then Blackstone ordered Abbott to shoot Rajah."

I pulled my sleeve over my hands to avoid leaving any fingerprints and turned the doorknob. To my amazement, the door was unlocked. I stepped inside of the bleak living room. Blood had sprayed across the dirty white couch. I closed my eyes to blot out the image of Abbott hesitantly pulling the trigger of the gun pressed up against the Winged One's head. I made my way past the murder scene into the tiny, brown kitchen. Each drawer had been pulled out as if someone was looking for something. I had no idea what I was looking for. Anything that would prove Blackstone's guilt. I didn't think the Welkies here would believe a ghost's testimony. That's when I noticed something high up on the refrigerator. "Fern, can you get that folder for me?"

The ghost levitated up and grabbed the old folder. She

came back down and looked around with a sad look in her eyes. "Rajah believed in me!" She handed me the folder with a distracted look in her eyes. "When no one was around, he would talk to me. Asked me how my day went. He told me he would help avenge my death." She gave a big sigh. "I'm going to miss him."

I looked at the article inside the folder. It was from the student newspaper about an alleged attack on a young librarian who committed suicide. Due to the many errors, the article must have been a rough draft that never went to print. The name shocked me as I looked up at the ghost. "Who attacked you, Fern?" I asked in a quiet voice.

She looked away from me as tears began to flow down her cheeks. They evaporated the moment they hit the linoleum floor. "Eddie warned me about him. He told me not to fall for him. I should've listened to Eddie." She began crying again, and much to my silent protest, she faded away.

I took a wild stab at guessing who the perpetrator was that committed the awful crime towards my newfound friend. After all these years, Fern still lived with the horror of Merrill Blackstone,

Junior, taking her life. Eddie was right about Blackstone. He was a maggot. I tucked the article away in the pocket of my jeans and put the folder back where I had found it.

Harriet wasn't in the room where I had left her. In fact, she was kneeling outside the mystery door. What was in her hand? She was inserting a long screwdriver in between the door and its frame. I quietly crept up beside her, not announcing my presence until I was right behind her. "Lost, Harriet?"

The screwdriver dropped to the ground. "Yeah—Well, no," the enchantress replied as she scooped it back up, "I think I might have locked myself out of our room when I went for a walk. I get frequent bouts of insomnia."

"Right," I said, not believing a word. "You do realize that this isn't our room?"

Harriet blushed. "How silly of me!" She grabbed my hand and nearly dragged me back to our unlocked room. Surprise, surprise!

Once we were back in our room, Harriet crawled into bed

and pretended to go to sleep, but I was on edge. Her actions lately didn't fit the profile of a nurse at a college campus clinic.

"So, what were you really doing with that screwdriver?" I demanded.

Harriet leaned against the wall. She took a deep breath. "Okay," she said after a few moments, "I'm not actually a nurse. I'm really a private investigator."

"That explains a lot."

Harriet seemed shocked. "You could tell?"

"No offense, but at the clinic, you seemed pretty stupid when it came to my injured nose."

She sighed. "Crap! I need to work on my aliases a lot more."

"To pardon the cliché, what's a P.I. like you doing in a place like this?"

She showed me her badge. "Remember that story I told you when you first came here? It was partly true. The old librarian was my aunt Thelma. A female ghost had told her that a murder had been committed here about forty years ago. When she went to President Blackstone with the information, he told her that she was hallucinating. No one, except for Rajah, would believe her. Finally, they dismissed Thelma on MTL, Mental Trauma Leave."

"Fern!"

"What?"

"Never mind, continue."

"Anyway, she told me about it, hired me to investigate, and I decided to go undercover as a nurse at the university's clinic."

"I thought you didn't believe in ghosts, Harriet."

She laughed. "Are you kidding? My cat, Inky, is a ghost cat. It was all part of my cover. And by the way, my name's not Harriet Legolas. It's really Brooke Luptin."

"Wait a minute! Do you know anything about nursing?"

"I took a community First Aid/CPR course."

Yeesh! So glad she wasn't a real nurse. "So, when you were in the library basement, you were doing some investigating?"

"You followed me down there?"

I nodded.

"Well, during my investigation, I learned one of the victims killed here was a student. So, I decided to look for a picture to see if Aunt Thelma could match her face to the ghost she saw."

"But you didn't," I said, reading the shocked look on her face. "After you left, I started looking through the yearbooks and came across a forty-year-old one with some of the pages cut out." The pieces were slowly forming together. Blackstone had attacked Fern and didn't want his record to be tarnished. So, he had the pages with her pictures cut out from the yearbook before the other students received them. But it still didn't make sense. Why were Eddie's photos missing and his existence here at Urbana College of Magic completely erased?

"I just wish we had something concrete to find out what really happened," Brooke/Harriet was saying.

"I've got something!" I jumped up and scrambled over to my suitcase. I pulled out the stack of papers that Robin had sent me. "Well, we've got at least one suspect. President Merrill Blackstone, Junior." I dropped the stack in her lap. "Apparently, he's not too well-liked by the ladies."

Brooke began looking through all the dirt on the President of the college. "Where did you get this?" she asked, amazed that I had access to such confidential information.

"My brother sent it to me," I explained.

She shook her head. "This information is good, but it looks like all the charges against him were dropped. I can't have Blackstone arrested on these reports alone. I need something more concrete."

I began racking my brain for an idea. I desperately wanted to help nail this slimeball, but Brooke was right. If she used any of these reports against the wizard, they would not be admissible in court because they were already dropped or dismissed. It might throw Blackstone's character into question, and all he would be charged with is a bad reputation. There was no way that I was going to suggest to Brooke that Fern take the stand and testify against her attacker. The ghost had been stuck in this hellhole for too long. Ghosts can't move from place to place if they have unfinished business with the living in the area where they died. The last thing the spirit needed before she could move freely was to face her killer in court. Then an idea hit me like a speeding Amtrak train. "What about the locked room down the hall? What's in there?"

"Aunt Thelma told me that the room supposedly holds a memory mirror. She remembered seeing President Blackstone go in there a couple of times, but the problem is the door is locked up tight as a drum. Believe me, I've tried to pry it open, but it looks like Blackstone put some kind of spell on the door."

Memory mirrors. That would be a perfect way to prove Blackstone's guilt. These magical devices look like mirrors at first glance, but a Welkie, by the use of a memory removal wand, can store about 1,000 selected memories in just one looking glass. I have heard that anyone can walk through the memory mirror and be instantly transported (as an observer only) into that person's memory.

"Look," Brooke was saying, "I have to meet with my aunt and supervisor tomorrow. If you don't mind, I'll show him these reports."

"Sure," I replied in a distracted voice. I was thinking about my lock picking skills I had acquired when I was a kid. Heck, I had used them to help one member of the undead, and I was almost positive that I could definitely help out his sister.

I decided not to make any attempt to break into the locked door while at work. Blackstone didn't need to know I was planning to look into his private memories on the clock. I barely paid attention to my work as my excitement was growing more and more with each passing hour.

The moment my shift ended at five, I rushed back to my room at breakneck speed. I was trembling so hard with excitement I nearly dropped the screwdriver Brooke/ Harriet had used the night before. Settle down, Shelly! Don't get your hopes up. Most likely, the memories would be reasonably dull.

I crept down the hall and faced the door clutching the screwdriver in my shaking hand. The moment I inserted the tool in one of the holes, it jerked back hard as it hit a wall of magical energy. I thought that I heard my shoulder pop out of its socket. No quitter's blood in me. I stuck the screwdriver in again, but this time, the screwdriver shot back as if a bolt of electricity ran through me. I let out a yelp of pain.

"Miss Anderson, you must really enjoy sticking your nose where it doesn't belong."

I swiftly picked up the screwdriver as I got to my feet to face the wizard, Merrill Blackstone. Or was he an evil sorcerer playing the part of a good wizard? "You're not supposed to be on the women's floor!"

"I am the President of this college. I can go anywhere I want." A sadistic grin spread across his face, twisting from a vain expression to an evil, egotistical one.

I definitely didn't want to be alone with him as he began to advance on me like a tiger stalking a baby gazelle. "Stay away from me, Mr. Blackstone!" I warned him as I waved the screwdriver like a weapon.

He threw back his head as a strangely gentle laugh escaped from his lips. "What are you afraid of, Miss Anderson? It's a shame that Rajah isn't here to protect you."

"If you come near me again, I'll call the campus police."

He smiled that evil smile again. "Miss Anderson, you do realize that I can arrange for your untimely death?"

"Like you arranged Rajah's suicide and the incidents with your past girlfriends?" I demanded.

His expression changed to one of pure anger and hatred. The president grabbed my wrist, but then he let go and folded up like a lawn chair after I kneed him right in the crotch. "You hussy!" he snarled at me as I ran past him.

I slammed my door, locking it behind me. I grabbed the chair from the desk and jammed it under the doorknob. That would not hold up against a Welkie's powers for very long, but right now, that was my only option. I hugged myself to stop the shivers of terror that were running up and down my spine. All I could do now was wait.

About an hour later, I was standing once again in front of the enchanted door. Blackstone was nowhere to be found. Fine by me. But there was one problem. I had no idea how to disengage the spell the worm put on the door. Not that Blackstone would have willingly told me the spell breaker in the first place. I tried kicking the door, but the energy knocked me onto my butt. "Ow!" I said.

"Need some help?" Fern suddenly appeared beside me. Reaching out a ghostly hand, she helped me to my feet. "Why are you trying to open that door?"

"I think there's something very important behind here, but the President has put a spell on it so it can't be opened."

The ghost looked away. She had been in the room, but couldn't bring herself to go through the memory mirror. "Don't go in there, please!" She got down on her knees and grasped my hand in an attempt to pull me away.

"Fern, take me through the door!" I ordered in a stern voice. "You don't have to go through the mirror, just through the door."

The ghost reluctantly took my hand, and I was suddenly lifted off the ground a few inches. "Close your eyes," she warned me.

I did as I was told. The first time I phased through a solid object was one of the best things I've ever experienced. A gentle surge of magical energy flowed through my body as if I was drinking a cup of hot chocolate on a cold, snowy day. We hovered through the air for only a moment or two, and then we settled on the floor.

I opened my eyes. "Wow!" I said. I had never felt us go through the door. I found myself standing in a small room with a low ceiling. A lone burning bulb attached to an old ceiling fan was the only light illuminating the stuffy room. Under the fan was a mirror with a purple frame, pulsating with strong magic. Fern had left the room just as quickly and quietly as we had come.

Here goes nothing, I told myself. I took a deep breath and stepped through the memory mirror.

Chapter Ten:
I Take a Look into Eddie's Past

I found myself in a dorm quite similar to mine but without

any signs of modern technology. Two sets of bunk beds, a

five-drawer bureau, and a desk were the only objects in the

cluttered room. A ten-gallon aquarium tank was sitting on the

desk with a black cloth halfway draped across it. Someone was

bent over, looking at the tank. The door swung open, and a much

younger Merrill Blackstone stormed inside. "Eddie, what did you

say to your sister?" he demanded.

The other man straightened himself up and turned around

to face the angry wizard. I gave a quick gasp. Eddie didn't have

any fangs, nor was his skin pale at all. In fact, he looked very

healthy. "Why? Because I told her the truth about you?" he

snapped. Even though I couldn't read Eddie's mind in this

warped world, I could feel the tension in his voice. "You're a disgusting playboy who doesn't care about a woman's feelings."

Blackstone looked shocked.

"You only use women to benefit your own selfish needs. I know how you stole the class election by sleeping with every woman! That's really low!"

Blackstone shrugged as he walked over to the desk. "I'm a Blackstone. I can do whatever I want." He opened a desk drawer and pulled out a vial of blood. He pulled back the cloth on the tank and popped open the cap. He swiftly poured the blood out on a small Petri dish just as a red lizard with black dots shot out from under a huge rock and across the floor of the grass-covered tank. Its black tongue licked up the blood in not more than a half-minute. "I see you were admiring my vampire lizard. Isn't it a beaut?"

Eddie shook his head in disbelief. "Why did you bring a vampire lizard on campus? What if it gets loose and turns someone into a vampire?"

"Then maybe you can use your vampire slayer skills like

your father taught you? Or are the rumors I hear true?"

"What rumors?" Eddie asked a little too defensively.

"You've become friends with vampires and aren't going to follow in Daddy's footsteps."

"I just don't think we should kill them. Vampires and Welkies aren't that much different from each other."

Blackstone smiled as if he understood. "Ah-ha! I get it now. You're studying business so you can infiltrate the bloodsuckers' community and then kill them."

"Whatever," Eddie answered with a non-committed shrug. "So, what did Fern say to you?

Blackstone's face twisted up in anger. "She lied to me!"

"Oh, please, Merrill! You really thought Fern wouldn't go to the dean after you stole her ethics paper."

"She helped me with the paper, and I passed. It wasn't stealing!"

"You passed her paper off as your own. You've done it before. As if you would ever turn in your own work."

"Fern will regret what she did to me."

Eddie looked at him with piercing green eyes. "You stay

away from my sister!" he warned. Then he gathered up a pair of red boxing gloves and a duffle bag and walked out of the room.

I wanted to run after my boyfriend for leaving me alone with Blackstone. Then I realized that I was only an observer in the sorcerer's memories. I watched as he pulled the cover back over the tank. "She will pay!" he told himself.

A purple swirling mist gathered me up and began spinning me around and around. I shut my eyes to keep the onset of dizziness away. When I opened my eyes, I realized that I was standing in the stacks of the library. I knew that I was still in Blackstone's memories because many of the books looked shiny and new as if they hadn't yet been touched by patrons' hands. Then I saw Fern all alone in the library shelving a couple of books.

"Hello, Fern," Blackstone said as he sauntered up to her. He placed a hand on her shoulder. "About yesterday, I think there must have been a little misunderstanding between us."

She pulled away from him. "Leave me alone!"

He reached out and grabbed her elbow. All the books dropped to the floor with a loud crash. "You don't ever threaten a member of the Blackstone family!" he snarled as he shoved her to the ground. The loud crack of bone echoed throughout the building. "You'll pay for this!" he growled.

"Merrill, don't!" Fern screamed.

The next time I opened my eyes, I was back in the men's dorm room. Blackstone was standing by the desk feeding his pet vampire lizard another vial of blood. The door almost swung off its hinges when Eddie stormed inside. His green eyes were ablaze with fury as he punched the other wizard in the nose, "You sick son of a hellhound!" Eddie snapped. An expression of shock crossed my face. To call someone a son of a hellhound was the worst insult that someone could lay upon another person. My boyfriend might as well have called Blackstone's mother a prostitute. I had never seen Eddie so angry at someone. "What did you do to my sister?"

"What do you mean?" Blackstone asked as a malicious smile crossed his lips.

"Don't give that crap, Merrill! I just got back from the clinic with Fern. You broke her arm, you filthy cur! You don't deserve to live!" Eddie lunged at Blackstone with all of his might. His fist hit Blackstone in the left eye. *Go get 'em, Eddie*, I silently cheered. *Kick his sorry butt!*

Blackstone tried to push him off, but Eddie had the advantage of being quicker than his roommate and was running on adrenaline-fueled anger. "She got what was coming to her!" Blackstone snarled. "Duracell!" A ball of black energy escaped from his fingers and knocked Eddie right into the tank.

Glass flew everywhere, including into Eddie's arm. Blood began seeping down his long-sleeved shirt and onto the floor. The young wizard opened his mouth in horror as he watched the vampire lizard dart towards him. "Merrill! Kill it before it bites me!" he pleaded. "Use a nebulae spell!"

Blackstone slowly stepped back. "Why should I?" he asked in a strangely calm voice.

Eddie's eyes widened in horror. The lizard fixed its unblinking eyes upon him before it leaped onto his shoulder. He let out an agonizing scream as the lizard sank its jaws into his flesh, leaving him completely immobile. The blood literally began to drain from his skin as it turned to a deathly pale color.

"Eddie!" I pleaded as tears began to run down my cheeks. He was in so much pain, and I wished that I could do something—anything—to help him. My feet were frozen in place. I had almost forgotten that I was in Blackstone's memories as an observer.

Blackstone smirked down at the dying wizard. "How does it feel to be rejected, Eddie? What would you like me to tell your dear sister? Before I get rid of the liar and her big mouth! Can't have her spreading the word on campus about what happened!"

Eddie opened his mouth to say something, but only air came out. No blood clotted around the wound. He began to go into violent convulsions for only a few moments. Then his eyes rolled to the back of his head, and he slumped to the floor, lifeless.

The lizard removed its venomous fangs from his shoulder and darted under the bureau. Its belly was full as it let out a satisfied hiss. Blackstone smiled admirably at the lizard. "Good work, my pretty!" He turned on his heel and left without looking back even once.

My feet were free, and I began running toward Eddie. I had almost reached him when, suddenly, the scene around me began to fade. "No!" I screamed. This was not happening! I couldn't leave my boyfriend after what that heartless hellhound did to him.

When I opened my eyes, I was standing on the edge of the balcony. Blackstone was up in Fern's face. "You won't ruin my future, you wench!" He grabbed Fern's wrist and began to twist.

"Let go! I'll tell—!" Fern shouted.

"Who?" Blackstone said in a mocking voice. "Eddie? He can't save you now!"

With her free hand, Fern raked her nails across his face. "Let go of me, you hellhound!" she screamed.

"Die you hag!" Blackstone screamed. He placed a hand over the young librarian's face and gave a violent shove.

Fern screamed as the railing broke into two. I watched in horror as she tumbled to the ground. The awful sound of breaking bones echoed throughout the library. I forced myself to peer over the railing and nearly threw up when I saw her twisted body lay on the floor as a pool of blood began forming around her head.

I suddenly felt someone stumble through me as if I was transparent. "Eddie, I thought you were dead?"

Eddie never heard me. He didn't seem to know what was going on as he mumbled incoherently to himself. He staggered over to the railing and screamed in horror the moment he saw Fern's body. "No!" He stood in shock as the horrible truth washed over him. Coming into the memory mirror was a big mistake. I had never wanted to see Eddie's painful past.

Blackstone rushed up to the shocked man and shoved him over the balcony. He did nothing as Eddie toppled to his death. For the second time in less than a few minutes, the ugly thud of a body hitting the floor rang throughout the building.

Then I heard the same sickening sound I heard when my mother died. Eddie's neck had snapped, and I knew that he was dead. I stared at Blackstone's remorseless face, and goosebumps blossomed all over my skin.

"Penicillin!" the murderer said as he touched the scratch marks on his face. They instantly disappeared. He smiled triumphantly as he sauntered down the stairs and over to the two side-by-side bodies. Then he used a levitation spell to move Fern's arm and let it rake across Eddie's throat. Blackstone was framing Eddie for Fern's death! I was too transfixed in horrified grief to notice the scene changing for the last time.

Where was I? I looked around at the small office. Blackstone was standing next to an older man who I surmised to be his father after reading the name on the desk plaque. They were talking to a very distraught person. Once I turned around, I was face-to-face with Eddie, who had been changed into a vampire. He had his head cupped in his hands as he sat in a black chair.

"What am I supposed to do? I know nothing about being a vampire! My mother will disown me like she did with my brother!"

he asked in a hysterical voice. "You can't kick me out! I didn't kill Fern, and if I did, I didn't mean to!" He attempted to wipe the tears that were now streaming down his cheeks.

"That's your problem, Edgar!" said Blackstone's father, coldly. "You turned yourself into a vampire and had a fight with your sister in the library. Merrill told me you brought the lizard here on campus!"

"No, that's not true!" Eddie screamed. "He's lying as always! Why don't you ask him about the genie fights and the paper he stole from my sister?"

"Don't raise your voice to me, vampire!" snapped the President. "Merrill never lies! He is an honest and trustworthy student. Why should I believe a vampire over my own son? You are hereby forbidden to ever set foot on Urbana College of Magic. Your records here will be permanently erased. Get out of my office, vampire!"

Eddie bowed his head in defeat and slowly walked out of the office. I barely heard Blackstone's father saying no record of the last night would ever be found. I followed my boyfriend and stumbled out of the memory mirror.

Once I realized that I was back in reality, I sank to the dirty, old floor and began to sob. Not for me, but for Eddie and all the hell and hurt he went through. The people here had ruined his life and swept the whole incident away as if nothing had happened. Something had happened. A young lady was attacked and murdered. Her brother was turned into a vampire by her killer, who then killed him. Two lives destroyed all because of one evil, black-hearted man who didn't get what he wanted.

Suddenly, I managed to get hold of myself when I heard a loud beeping over the building's PA system. An automated voice came on, saying, "Code Blood! Code Blood in the library!" Somewhere in the back of my mind, I remembered reading in the campus policy manual, it was the code for a vampire on the premise. Eddie! I ran to the door and gave the knob a hard, forceful kick. The spell must have worn off because the door swung open.

Chapter Eleven
A Deadly College Reunion

Blackstone ambushed me the second I walked out of the room. He grabbed me by the elbow and said, "Travel library!" White smoke surrounded us as I tried to break free from the sorcerer's grip. He had learned his lesson and was staying far away from me. The hallway disappeared before us, and I found Blackstone and myself teleported to the campus library.

I performed a foot sweep and knocked Blackstone on his rear. He let go of me, allowing me to run up the balcony stairs. I know, stupid horror film move, but Blackstone must have hit the hidden button that closed off the entire building to outsiders, and there was no place else to run. "You think you can run from me, Ms. Anderson? I am a powerful wizard, and you are just a mere mortal and a loose end I need to clean up."

I made it to the balcony with Blackstone right on my heels. I looked around for a weapon, anything to defend myself. Out of the corner of my eye, I saw Fern push a metal bookend to me. Perfect! Blackstone tended to use magic a lot more than logic, so I surprised him when I nailed him upside the head with the metal bookend. He staggered back with the same confusion that Aquaman has whenever he is on land.

"You think you're so smart!" I challenged him. "But I know you've been stealing money from the library's funds to fund your illegal genie fights!"

"How do you know about that?"

"I saw how you forced Abbott to kill the green genie, Dreyson."

His face paled a bit. "That was over thirty years ago. You couldn't have been there." He staggered back in surprise. "What are you?"

"The librarian who is going to bring you down."

"You'll pay—!" Blackstone was cut off in mid-sentence when a hand spun him around and gave him a powerful uppercut to the jaw, knocking the wizard back on the ground. "Eddie Van

Helsing?" he asked. "What are you doing here?"

Within seconds, Eddie pulled his Scorpion XL, a high

powered handgun that fired off rounds of laser bullets, out from

its hip holster, and pointed it directly at Blackstone's head. The

vampire had loaded the gun before he stepped on campus, and I

wasn't quite sure if he was planning on using the bullets. "You

keep your slimy hands away from my girlfriend!" he snarled at

Blackstone.

The beads of sweat were pouring down the wizard's

cheeks as though the Hoover Dam had just broken. He wiped

away the blood oozing from his lips. "What are you going to do

with me, Eddie?" The question was supposed to be cocky, but it

came out in a whimper. "Suck the blood out of me?"

"Shut up!" My boyfriend's voice became low but extremely

dangerous.

"I—You haven't changed much since the last time I saw

you."

"You sorry excuse of a wizard!" Eddie growled as his

finger tightened on the trigger. "You think I like being a vampire,

Merrill? You think that I like not being able to go outside in the sun for more than an hour? You ruined one part of my life. I won't let you destroy the rest of it!"

Blackstone glanced over in my direction. "Is that your so-called girlfriend?" he snarled as he suddenly got his confidence back. "She's just like your sister!"

Eddie moved his gun a little to the left and fired. The bullet hit the floor just inches from Blackstone's head. "Don't you dare talk about Fern that way!" he growled. Without taking his eyes off his old roommate, the vampire said, "Shelly, get out of here!"

I had moved behind the vampire and was about to leave when I read his mind. "No!" I said, frantically shaking my head.

"Shelly, leave now!"

I placed a hand on my boyfriend's arm. "Don't do it, Eddie! Killing him won't bring your sister back."

There was a long pause, but Eddie never lowered his gun. "No, but it will give me satisfaction."

"Eddie, please!" I said.

Unfortunately, this gave Blackstone enough time to

retaliate. He uncapped the blue bottle and mouthed the word, "Abbott!"

Eddie pulled me close to him as a swirling cloud of blue-green smoke appeared in the room. POOF! The purple genie, Abbott, stood directly in front of us. "Yes, master?" he asked Blackstone in a hissing voice.

"Get rid of these people for me!" Blackstone ordered the genie.

The genie turned towards us and morphed into the creature I had seen in the basement. A blue streak of light shot out of its mouth.

Eddie and I dropped to the ground and rolled out of the way. This genie wasn't going to kill my boyfriend and me. Not if I could help it. I flipped through my mental filing cabinet to remember what Abbot had told me. The bottle! I had to get a hold of that bottle. The formulating plan in my mind certainly was a crazy one with a very slim chance of success, but that was a risk I was going to have to take.

I glanced up from my position on the carpeted floor to see the flowered glass bottle only a foot away from Blackstone's side. I crawled army-style toward Blackstone, and before anyone had time to react, I grabbed the bottle. I pulled myself to my feet and hung the bottle over the edge of the balcony. "Hey, Abbott!"

The genie faced me and was about to blast me with another deadly light ray.

"Give it up, Blackstone, or I'll drop the bottle!"

Blackstone must have thought I was kidding around. "Destroy them, Abbott!"

I threw the bottle off the balcony. Pieces of colored glass scattered across the floor the second it hit the ground. The Blackstone brand tattoo began to fade away as Abbott's shape-shifting tattoo glowed brighter and brighter. Abbott nodded a silent thanks before turning to the wizard. "You!" he roared.

Blackstone began to crawl backward in horror. "Abbott, my faithful servant—."

"Don't patronize me, you worthless piece of mortal trash!" the genie snarled. "I have served you and your despicable family for generations with the promise of freedom. But what do I get in return? Nothing! Absolutely nothing!" As the genie spoke, he morphed into various, purple creatures I have seen only in my darkest nightmares.

"But, but—!" Blackstone stammered.

"Don't speak!" Abbott ordered as he changed for the final time into a ten-foot-tall Sasquatch with purple fur. He grabbed the wizard by the collar of his shirt. "You forced me to hurt all those women, and you had me kill the janitor. 'Loose ends' you called them. To cover up your lying, cheating ways!"

"I can make things better. I'll make sure no one ever finds out about your crimes!"

The genie gave a rueful laugh. "You're right! No one will find out."

Eddie and I watched in stunned horror as the genie rammed his hand into Blackstone's face. We both winced as every facial bone shattered. The vampire still had his gun drawn but took his finger off the trigger. He knew better than to threaten an angry, powerful genie.

Abbott slung the unconscious, possibly dead wizard over his shoulder like a sack of dirty laundry, and looked at us. "Thank you for freeing me.”

“You’re welcome,” I said cautiously.

“I won’t hurt you, but if you try to follow me, you will die.” He snapped his fingers and disappeared in a cloud of smoke.

“Shelly,” said a voice behind us. We turned around to see Brooke with her gun drawn. The look of bewilderment raced across her face. “Where did Blackstone go? The police are on their way.”

Eddie and I looked at each other, silently debating what we should tell her. I finally decided on the truth while the vampire returned the gun back to its hip holster. I told Brooke what had transpired here in the library. “And then they both left in a puff of smoke.”

“Do you know where they went?”

“I do.”

“Where?” Brooke and Eddie asked at the same time.

“Wishteria.”

“Oh!” Brooke said in understanding.

“Wishteria is the genie homeworld,” I explained. “To get

there, a wormhole has to be opened, and if you go there, there is a very slim chance of survival. Abbott told me about it."

Brooke blew out a sigh. "Great, just great! What am I supposed to tell the cops when they get here?"

I managed a smile. "Well, you have a lot of physical evidence against Blackstone if he ever shows up. He does have the memories of the murder in a memory mirror stored in the last room on the left on the woman employees' floor."

Later on, I walked back to my room with Eddie as the fresh evening air blew past us. He looked around at all the buildings, wistfully. "Wow! Things have really changed here!" he said. He pointed to a window in the men's dormitory. "That used to be my room when I went to school here."

"I know. I've been in your old room."

Eddie gave me a curious look as we sat down together on the wall. "Back there with Blackstone, did you really see his memories?" he asked me.

I nodded slowly. What I saw was horrible, and I certainly didn't want to think about it. I leaned my head against him. "I even saw how you became a vampire. It was one of the worst things I've ever seen."

"You know the last time I saw Fern was her twisted body on the library floor. For forty years, I haven't been able to erase that memory from my mind." He didn't say it aloud, but he longed to see his sister one last time.

"Eddie?" a familiar voice asked. A transparent hand touched his shoulder.

He looked up in absolute disbelief as the ghost floated in front of us. "Fern, is that really you?"

Fern nodded.

Eddie searched my face for the truth. "It's really her!" I said as a few tears started to roll down my cheeks. This was going to be the best thing that had happened ever since I arrived at the college.

The vampire got up and gave the ghost a great big hug. "I've missed you so much." His voice cracked with emotion. Tears began to fill his eyes.

"Me too, Eddie," Fern replied.

I sat back and enjoyed the long silence between brother and sister. A huge lump was starting to form in my throat at the happy reunion.

Finally, they let go of each other. Eddie looked up and down at his little sister. "You're not staying here," he said in a big-brother voice. "You're coming to live with Dirk and me."

"Dirk? How is he?"

A fanged smile spread across Eddie's face. "He's doing great and will be very happy to see you. Once I help Shelly pack her things, we can get out of here." He took my hand and pulled me to my feet.

As we walked back to the apartment, I let Fern and Eddie talk. Apparently, the ghost had kept all the various newspaper articles written about Eddie when he was an undercover agent and a bounty hunter in one great big box. The second box had keepsakes about Dirk when he was a semi-famous rock musician, which I didn't know. Even after they had become vampires, Fern still respected her big brothers and looked up to them. It was the same way I've looked up to my brother.

It took me only about a half-hour to pack. Eddie and Fern had taken my other two bags out to his car. Just as I had finished zipping up the laptop case, Brooke came into our room. Her hair was pulled back into a tight ponytail and stuffed under a navy blue ball cap. She had lost the ugly glasses, which I now knew were for her undercover job. "Hey, Shelly," she said, "I want to let you know that we confiscated President Blackstone's memory mirror. Too bad we couldn't nab him."

I shrugged. After what I had seen with the town and college, that didn't surprise me one bit. "I think wherever Blackstone is, he is paying for all of his crimes. Abbott apparently saw to that."

"Do you think that Blackstone's dead?"

"Most likely."

"At least it's less paperwork for us." She started to leave, but I stopped her as I rummaged through my purse for a piece of paper. I quickly jotted two email addresses and two phone numbers. "The first email and phone number are mine, and the other two belong to my brother. If you're ever in Zephyr, look us up, especially Robin. He really wants to meet you!"

Brooke smiled. "I'll definitely do that." She reached out and shook my hand. "Thanks for putting up with me and my undercover work."

I returned the smile and the handshake. "It was interesting." We exchanged good-byes, and I headed out the door.

When I reached Eddie's car, I immediately curled up in the backseat. Fern was up in front, still talking to her brother. It didn't bother me. It had been a long, tiring day, both emotionally and physically. I shut my eyes and quickly fell into a peaceful sleep.

Chapter Twelve
Eddie and I Have a Long Overdue Talk

A week had passed before I saw Eddie again. I thought it was best to let him spend a week alone, catching up with his sister. Amelia and Dad liked the invitation template that I had finally finished. This was a good thing because I wasn't about to spend another five hours working on another model. At least I only had to do one drawing instead of five hundred.

Everybody asked me how my time at Urbana College of Magic went, but I either avoided the question or sidestepped the answer. The last day there had been pretty bad, and the last thing I wanted to do was blab Eddie's past to the entire Zephyr community. He would've done the same for me.

On Friday, I got a phone call from Eddie. We were going

to have a moonlit picnic on the beach. At exactly six o'clock, he arrived at my house on his motorcycle. "Hey, babe!" the vampire greeted me with a wide grin as I walked out to the bike. He gave me a peck on the cheek. "All set?"

"Yeah!" I climbed on the back of the green motorcycle. A chilly night breeze blew past me as I wrapped my arms around myself. I should have grabbed a light jacket or a sweatshirt.

"Shelly, open up the box," Eddie said as a twinkle appeared in his green eyes. "I have a little something for you."

I opened the lid on the box and saw a miniature picnic basket inside. Eddie had shrunk the basket to make room next to it for the light green hooded sweatshirt with the words Tally's written across the front in white lettering. Tally's was a costly department store I could only dream of shopping at. I pulled it over my head. "This is cute, Eddie! Wherever did you find it?" I asked as it warmed my cold body. I unbuckled the extra helmet from the side rails and put it on.

"Actually, it's a thank-you gift from Fern," Eddie said as he started up the motorcycle.

"Oh, she didn't have to."

"She insisted. It was the least she could do."

I wanted to ask him how his sister was doing, but I decided that it could wait until we got to our destination. I wrapped my arms around Eddie's waist just as the motorcycle started to speed down the road. I leaned against his back, feeling the safest I had felt ever since I had stepped on the college campus.

Eddie parked the motorcycle in the parking lot by the beach and grabbed the tiny picnic basket. He set it on the sandy pavement and brought it back to its normal size with a "Maximum five!" I took his hand as he grabbed the wicker basket handles with the other hand. "You pick the spot, Shell!"

With the help of the bright moonlight, I picked out a soft sandy area a few feet away from the shore's edge. "That spot over there looks great!" I said as I took off my sandals so I could walk in the sand. "Take off your shoes, Eddie."

"Okay," Eddie said, humoring me. He slipped off his socks and shoes. "Ready?"

We walked along the cool, snow-white sand, hand-in-hand, to the spot I had picked out. After we put down our shoes and the basket, I rolled up my pant legs and pulled Eddie to the edge of the water. We stood ankle-deep in the ocean as the water pulled back and forth around us. "So," I finally asked, "how's Fern doing?" We started walking along the beach and headed back to the basket.

"Good!" Eddie replied. He unfolded a white bed sheet onto the sand and then helped me as I got out the two peanut butter and jelly sandwiches, bottled water, and a bag of tortilla chips and salsa.

"I've wanted to ask you some questions, Eddie, about your past. Are you up to answering them?"

The vampire nodded reluctantly.

I swallowed hard. "First, I think I should tell you what I saw in the memory mirror," I told him everything as I put my arm around his waist. I sensed that he needed someone to talk to. When I read his mind, I realized that for all these years, my boyfriend had blamed himself for his sister's death. "Fern's death wasn't your fault, Eddie." I placed a hand on his shoulder to console him.

Eddie was silent for a long time after I had finished. "I know that now, but I still should have stopped it somehow." Tears began to stream down his cheeks as he let out all that hidden self-blame. A few minutes later, he stopped crying and managed to smile at me. "At first, I was furious at you for digging into my past, but now I'm happy you did." The vampire wiped away his remaining tears. "You reunited me with my sister." He leaned over me and gave me a kiss on the top of my head. We were silent for a few moments. "Everything's all right now. What did you want to ask me?"

"Well, why did you start your undergrad classes so late in life?"

He swallowed hard. "Do you really want to know the answer to that?"

I nodded.

He sighed. "I come from a long line of vampire slayers. For many years, I was trained intensively to kill vampires. You saw the prejudice in Urbana. That was what was drilled into my head as I was growing up. But it was during the training that I realized what I was doing. I was supposed to enter vampires' homes and kill every family member, even little kids. I couldn't bring myself to kill them. The whole idea made me sick. I quit training and went to college to study business."

"Why didn't you tell me this?"

"My past isn't something I talk about. I didn't know what your reaction would be." He paused. "I didn't want to lose you."

I was silent for a long time as I grappled with Eddie's fears of losing me. I thought about how Blackstone treated Abbott. "Did your family ever own a genie?"

Eddie shook his head. "The Van Helsings may have been radicals, but we were never slave owners."

We were silent for a long time, and then I spoke. "When you were standing in front of Blackstone's father, you mentioned your mother would disown you like she did with Dirk. Did she?"

"Most Welkies in Urbana are high-class racists. They consider the undead lower-class citizens. My family was one of them. After Dirk became a vampire—."

"How did he become one? Or is that a sensitive subject,

too?"

Eddie gave a small laugh. "Actually, an old girlfriend of his turned him into one. Once Mom learned her oldest son had willingly become a vampire, she disowned Dirk and told me that I had to take care of the family."

I took a bite out of my PB&J. "Where was your father?" I asked.

"My father had died in battle when I was eight. When I went back to my mother's after I had been turned, she didn't even acknowledge me. The college had called her, and she immediately disowned me."

"Have you ever tried talking to her?"

Eddie shook his head sadly. "I've tried on several occasions, but she still refuses to talk to me." He finally took a bite of his sandwich.

"What did you do after that?"

"I lived on the streets for about a week until a wizard by the name of David Endora found me. Great guy! You should meet him sometime." He smiled fondly at the memories and then got back on track. "Anyway, I was very sick at the time because I wasn't able to drink any blood. David nursed me back to health, taught me how to cope with being a vampire, and set me up with some people who worked in intelligence." He gave a rueful laugh. "My slayer training did help me when I was a spy for the Agency."

"What is the Agency really?"

"An international group of spies and assassins. We basically infiltrated wherever we were needed. One of my home bases was right here in Zephyr."

"How long did you work for them?"

"About twenty-five years. After I quit, I became a bounty hunter for about ten years. I came back to Zephyr about eight years ago after finding out that Dirk was deejaying here, and did some odd jobs until I began working for your dad."

"Wow! I never realized how much you moved around."

He smiled. "Yeah, I was a pretty restless person."

"Was?"

"Until I met someone who has become very special to me."

Then I remembered something which had been lingering in the back of my mind for the past week. "Are your Uncle Konrad and Aunt Phoebe really related to you?"

Eddie shook his head. "Actually, I met them through Dirk. Uncle Konrad and Aunt Phoebe took me in." He paused before speaking again. "You're the first person I have told about my past in a really long time."

There was a long silence between us after Eddie finished up his story. I nodded as I took in everything that my boyfriend had told me. All these details about his past were fairly overwhelming for me. He had entrusted me with something only a few people knew. This was a big step forward in our relationship. The only sound that could be heard was the gentle lapping of the waves against the shore.

While I pondered these things, we lay back on the sheet and stared up into the night sky. Eddie drew me close to him and whispered in my ear. "I've got another secret. This one I've wanted to tell you." He paused dramatically and said in a sincere voice. "I love you, Shelly."

"I love you, too, Eddie." With that announcement, a loving,

passionate kiss seemed appropriate.

COMING SOON!

Carnival of the Undead
My Life among the Undead:
Book Four

Shelly Anderson has seen a lot of creepy people at the Zephyr Public Library where she is an assistant librarian, and now one of those people is stalking her. Even Shelly is not safe at the carnival when the stalker shows up with an army of zombie clowns. As if that's not stressful enough, her winged horse is seriously injured and someone has stolen a forbidden book on necromancy from the library. With the help of her boyfriend, Eddie Van Helsing, Shelly must find a way to stop her creepy, but elusive stalker with as few surprises as possible.

About the Author

Camara Bragdon has her master's degree in library and information science and lives in Maine. This is the third book in her vampire series, *My Life among the Undead*. Visit her at www.camarambragdonauthor.com